THE PORCUPINE, OR GAAG, POINTS HIS INTREPID SNOUT TO THE WEST WHERE HE BLUNDERED INTO THE LIVES OF OMAKAYAS'S FAMILY AND ACCOMPANIED THEM ON THEIR YEAR OF ADVENTURE, 1852, WHICH EVER AFTER, THE FAMILY REFERRED TO

AS: THE PORCUPINE YEAR

ode'imin
heart berry
BEARS LIKE BERRIES, TOO!

HERE MEMEGWESIWAG GUIDED THE FATE OF QUILL AND OMAKAYAS

THROUGH THESE MANY LAKES AND RIVERS, SWAMPS AND STREAMS, THE FAMILY MADE THEIR WAY

LAKE SUPERIOR

THE ISLAND OF THE GOLDEN BREASTED WOODPECKER

(WHERE THEY CAME FROM)

THE PORCUPINE YEAR

ALSO BY LOUISE ERDRICH

FOR CHILDREN

The Birchbark House

Grandmother's Pigeon

ILLUSTRATED BY JIM LAMARCHE

The Range Eternal

ILLUSTRATED BY STEVE JOHNSON AND LOU FANCHER

The Game of Silence

NOVELS

Love Medicine

The Beet Queen

Tracks

The Bingo Palace

Tales of Burning Love

The Antelope Wife

The Last Report on the Miracles at Little No Horse

The Master Butchers Singing Club

Four Souls

The Painted Drum

The Plague of Doves

WITH MICHAEL DORRIS

The Crown of Columbus

POETRY

Jacklight

Baptism of Desire

Original Fire

NONFICTION

The Blue Jay's Dance

Books and Islands in Ojibwe Country

LOUISE ERDRICH

THE
PORCUPINE
YEAR

HARPERCOLLINS*PUBLISHERS*

Library of Congress Cataloging-in-Publication Data
Erdrich, Louise.
The porcupine year / Louise Erdrich. — 1st ed.
    p.   cm.
Summary: In 1852, forced by the United States government
to leave their beloved Island of the Golden-Breasted
Woodpecker, fourteen-year-old Omakayas and her Ojibwe
family travel in search of a new home.
ISBN 978-0-06-029787-9 (trade bdg.)
ISBN 978-0-06-029788-6 (lib. bdg.)
1. Ojibwa Indians—Juvenile fiction. [1. Ojibwa Indians—
Fiction. 2. Indians of North America—Superior, Lake,
Region—Fiction. 3. Family life—Superior, Lake, Region—
Fiction. 4. Voyages and travels—Fiction. 5. Superior, Lake,
Region—History—19th century—Fiction.] I. Title.
PZ7.E72554Por 2008   2008000757
[Fic]—dc22   CIP
                                                       AC

1 2 3 4 5 6 7 8 9 10
❖
First Edition

For Nenaa'ikiizhikok

Kiizh, my little blue

CONTENTS

THE PORCUPINE YEAR

PROLOGUE

Here follows the story of a most extraordinary year in the life of an Ojibwe family and of a girl named Omakakiins, or "Omakayas," Little Frog, who lived a year of flight and adventure, pain and joy, in 1852, when the uncut forests of Minnesota still stretched, full and deep, west from the shores of Lake Superior.

Her family's journey began in a place we now know as Madeline Island. Like so many Ojibwe and other Native Americans, Omakayas's family were sent from their home by the United States government, to make way for European settlers. As they plunged into the great world, searching for a new home, a place where they could live in peace and never be removed, the family never forgot their old home. Madeline Island, the Island of the Golden-Breasted Woodpecker, was a beloved place and would never leave their hearts.

ONE

NIGHT HUNTING

Bekaa! Bekaa!

Omakayas froze and held tight to her paddle with one hand. She was trying to keep the canoe absolutely still while her younger brother, Pinch, balanced with his bow and arrow. With the other hand she held a torch of flaming pine pitch. *Wait, higher!* Omakayas and her brother had inched close to an old buck deer onshore. Eyes glowing, it gazed, curious and still, into the light of their torch. Omakayas's arm ached, trying to keep the canoe braced in the river's current. But she heard the faint high-pitched creak of the bow as her brother drew back the string and arrow, and she did not move one muscle, even when a drop of blistering pitch fell onto her arm. *Tsssip! Tonggg!* The arrow flew, the bowstring quivered.

Hiyn! Hiyn! Aaargh!

As the deer crashed through the trees, Pinch shouted in rage and disappointment.

"Your fault! You let us drift!"

Pinch dropped his bow with a clatter and jerked around to blame his sister, rocking the boat. Indignant and offended, Omakayas relaxed her arms. The canoe swerved, the torch wavered, and over the edge went Pinch. His thunking splash resounded through the trees onshore and made further night hunting worthless. Pinch came up spouting water—late spring runoff. The icy cold doused some of his heat, but he was still mad and ready to fight, especially once Omakayas hooted at him, laughing at the way he had gone over the side, arms out, flailing. She put out the torch with a hiss and expertly guided the canoe just out of his reach. Although they were allowed to go out night hunting, they were not supposed to go far from their family's camp.

"My fault, 'na? Do you want a ride or not?"

Pinch tried to lunge through the water at her, but Omakayas paddled just beyond his grasp.

"Remember what Deydey said? A good hunter never blames another for a missed shot."

Pinch stopped, treading water, his dark round head just barely visible in the moonlight. All of a sudden, he was tugged farther downstream.

"Hey!"

Pinch yelled in surprise just as Omakayas felt the canoe move toward him, as though propelled by an unseen hand.

"Watch out, the current's . . ." His words were swept off. Although Omakayas dug her paddle into the water, stroking backward, the canoe sped smoothly along, so fast that she caught up to Pinch immediately. Desperate to save him now, she stretched and held out the paddle for him to grasp. He pulled himself in, seriously frightened, and scrambled for his own paddle. But the moment had cost them and now the current was even stronger, ripping along the bank. The river abruptly widened and there was no question of turning around—all they could do was desperately try to slow and guide themselves away from the knots and snags of uprooted trees in the river's flow. These would loom suddenly, only faintly lighted by the moon. The great floating trees were moving too, Omakayas and Pinch realized. Slower and more grandly, perhaps, but they were only half hooked together. They were dangerous structures in what had become a singing flood. The children soon realized that they'd been tugged into the confluence of two rivers. Theirs had been slow and meandering, but the second river was carrying spring debris from a powerful rain far upstream. Not only that, but as they swept through the dark faster and faster they heard, ahead, the unmistakable roar of a rapids.

No sooner did they hear the rapids, and cry out, than the canoe leaped forward like a live thing.

There was no thinking. All went dark. They were rushing through the night on water they couldn't navigate, past invisible rocks, between black shores. All they could do was swallow their screams and paddle for their lives. Paddle with a wild strength they never knew they had between them. Omakayas felt the cold breath of the rocks as their canoe swept inches from a jagged edge, a monstrous jutting lip, a pointing finger of rough stone. As she paddled she cried out for the rocks, the asiniig, to guide them. Asked them in her mind and then called out again. They seemed to hear her. Even in the dark, she could see the rocks suddenly, areas of greater density and weight. Now she flew past them with a flick of her paddle. Steered by instinct. They hissed in her ears and she shifted balance, evaded. Their canoe didn't seem to touch the water. It was as though it had sprouted wings and was shooting down the rapids like a hawk swooping from the sky—and they landed the way a hawk would, too. Brought up in a sudden eddy. An upsweep of calm. But no sooner had they taken a breath than they were snatched back into the roar.

This time, the rapids sent them through a dark tunnel that seemed timeless, blind, malevolent. A yawning throat of water. The paddles flew from their grip. They twirled and spun in a sickening vortex. Moonless, mindless, they could only hold each other in the bottom of the canoe and wait for death.

As they held each other, falling or flying, Omakayas's one regret was that she'd laughed at Pinch as he fell from the canoe.

"I'm sorry," she cried out. He must have heard her because he yelled in grief and terror, "My sister, I'm sorry, too!"

Even in the chaos, Omakayas was amazed, trying to remember if Pinch had ever apologized to her before. But then the water threw them at each other like two young buffalo—they butted heads and saw winking lights, then nothing. Only blackness.

There was a sudden, eerie silence.

"Are we dead?" Pinch's voice quavered.

The blackness was so intense they could almost touch it. They were now hardly moving. They still held tightly to the sides of the canoe, but the water had suddenly let go of them. Or perhaps Pinch was right and they were dead, thought Omakayas. Perhaps they were entering the spirit world. But now the clouds lifted and a faint radiance spread around them. They looked at each other—still alive! They continued forward on what was now only a lazy lake current. Dazed, they raised themselves to look. The water spread all around them, glimmering in the calm blue moonlight. A black band of trees stretched out behind them and to the sides, but before them they could see nothing but more blackness and depth. So Omakayas and Pinch turned around and began to paddle toward what they marked as the eastern shore, under the eastern stars.

They scraped through the water with their hands, taking turns, warming their frozen palms and fingers in their armpits, digging into the water again. It seemed to take forever, but gradually the band of trees grew wider, the shore got closer, the water diminished, and they saw sand, logs, beach. By the time they dragged themselves onto land they were beyond exhaustion. And they were cold, very cold.

"Do you have your striker?" asked Pinch, touching the freezing sand.

Omakayas felt for her fire maker. Like her mother and grandmother, who were capable Anishinabe women, she always carried a flint and striker. She could start a fire anywhere with the stone and steel from the small pouch, which was still tied to her waist. But they were in unknown country now and did not want to be discovered.

"I don't know if we should have a fire," she whispered back. "There may be enemies."

As they pulled their canoe ashore with numb hands, Pinch said forlornly, "I wonder where we are."

"Saa. We should be quiet," said Omakayas. "We should hide the canoe."

"I don't see any fires through those trees, I don't smell any camps," said Pinch in a normal voice.

Still, they pulled the canoe into a stand of birch and

tipped it over. The canoe was always a handy shelter. They crawled beneath it and scraped together beds out of a pile of leaves. They had no blankets, nothing dry. But once they huddled together, in spite of the cold, they felt drowsy. In a few moments they were drifting into sleep, worn out, spent, but grateful with relief. Omakayas opened her eyes once, remembered, put her hand down through the leaves, and grasped a little rock.

"Thank you, miigwech," she said to it, before she closed her eyes again.

TWO

PORCUPINE SOUP

As she floated toward morning, underneath the canoe, Omakayas put her sleepy fingers on the beads at her throat. She was dreaming of Nokomis, her grandmother. Nokomis had worn these red beads ever since Omakayas could remember. One day, she had put her arms around her granddaughter and said, "My girl, you are becoming strong and generous. You are going to become a woman sometime this year. I give you my red beads."

"What do I get?" Pinch had asked. "I'm fearless, handsome, and truly kind!"

"Here, chew this," said Nokomis, and she'd given him a strip of dried meat.

Pinch was delighted. "You can't eat beads," he said, walking off with his mouth full.

Now, dream and memory mixed, and Omakayas touched the smooth, round beads at her throat. Maybe her red beads were going to be useful? Or maybe Pinch was just hungry. That was a sure bet!

Omakayas was no longer a little girl. She was that creature somewhere between a child and a woman—a person ready to test her intelligence, her hungers. A dreamer who did not yet know her limits. A hunter, like her brother, who was beginning to possess the knowledge of all that moved and breathed. A friend who did not know how far her love might extend. A daughter who still winced at her mother's commands and who loved and shyly feared her distant father. A girl who'd come to know something of her strength and who wanted challenge, and would get it, in the years of her family's exile from their original home—the Island of the Golden-Breasted Woodpecker.

That place was in her heart, even now, as she touched the red beads at her throat and began to wake so far away, curled for warmth next to her irritating brother.

"Puuu, hiyn! You stink!" She rolled away from him toward the crack of light under the canoe. Lifting the canoe's edge warily, she examined the shore. Empty. Gingerly, she crawled out. Behind her, Pinch was waking grumpily.

"How can I stink if I was washed in a crazy rapids? You're the one who stinks."

This was just normal talk with them and didn't mean anything at all. The two had started their days together with mild insults even before they left the island. To speak pleasantly to each other would have shocked the whole family. A family both of them missed very much at this moment.

Pinch crawled out from under the canoe, too. His hair, stiff and wiry, stuck in all directions. He was an unusually strong boy, which was why he had tested his strength with the bow, and also tested his sister's patience by hunting at night.

"I wish we were back on the island," he said, sighing with self-pity. "At least I'd know where we were!"

Suddenly he popped his eyes out at Omakayas, who laughed. Despite his troublesome ways, Pinch could always make her laugh. Plus he was a practical boy and was already planning how to get back to his family—he was, after all, very hungry.

"Let's just walk back," he said. "We'll go along the river."

"And leave our canoe?"

"It's old!"

"Gaawiin, it's still good!"

"It's heavy!"

"You big baby! Deydey and Old Tallow made it. Nokomis finished it off. What do you think they'll say if we leave it?"

"We'll come back for it."

But Omakayas was stubborn and refused to leave the canoe behind, even though they'd be unable to paddle it up the roaring stream and would have to carry it through the heavy growth by the river.

"Pinch, there's no choice. We must portage the canoe back to camp. They'll be waiting."

"Well, of course they'll wait for us," said Pinch, hurt. "Mama couldn't get along without me."

"You mean me," said Omakayas.

"Do we have anything to eat?"

Pinch's voice was small and wistful; he sounded like a little boy, not the warrior he pretended to be. He sat down on a log, looking out over the lake, and scratched his head. Then he threw himself onto the ground and groaned. "I'm getting weak."

Omakayas looked around them. She still had her woman's knife, secure in its beaded sheath at her belt, along with her fire-steel. Sometimes she carried loops of sinew along with the knife, but she'd already checked and found that she had none. She could have used the sinew to set a snare, maybe catch a rabbit, roast it if they got brave enough to make a fire. Her mouth watered at the thought. She was hungry, too. She went to the lake, put her face down to the clear surface, and admired the tiny colored pebbles on the bottom. She cupped her hands and drank, then smoothed her hair back and rebraided it quickly.

"If you're trying to make yourself beautiful," Pinch called, "give up, it's no use, come on back. I see breakfast!"

"What?"

Omakayas scrambled back to Pinch's log, where he was still lying flat on the ground, looking up into the trees. He pursed his lips up and pointed with this gesture into the budding leaves. Tucked into the crook of a branch, a porcupine, or gaag, rested. It was only a baby but looked quite plump and would certainly be tender, stewed up in a porcupine soup.

"All we have to do is knock it from the tree," said Pinch in a pleased voice. "I'm just lying here trying to do it with my thoughts."

"That could take a while, brother," said Omakayas. "Your thoughts are feeble. I think we should try a stick."

"Good idea!"

Pinch got up, his hair now even wilder, full of leaves, and the two searched the fringe of woods until they found a good long stick that would serve as a knocking pole. Pinch climbed into the lower branches of the tree, then edged himself up a little higher, and Omakayas fed the pole up to him. The gaag was still sleeping. It made no move to get away from them. The gaag's main protection is of course its quills, and not many animals will climb after them to eat them. Pinch's poking stick surprised the baby—it opened its little black eyes and then tried to dig its claws into the bark. After a few more jabs and pushes, the stick sent the gaag tumbling down—unfortunately, the porcupine bounced off Pinch.

"Yii, yii, oyii!!!"

Omakayas heard her brother's screams of pain, but she ignored them in order to get the porcupine. She rushed to the creature as soon as it landed, turned it over with a shorter stick, and prepared to plunge her knife swiftly into its soft underbelly and heart. A gaag has a sweet, trusting, bewildered little face and this one was so small—she didn't really like to end its life. She paused. But Omakayas was very hungry, so she lifted her knife. The gaag breathed out and closed its eyes, as if it knew it was doomed.

Pinch climbed down from the tree, whimpering a little, and cried, "Stop!"

Omakayas froze and took her knife away from the creature.

"Sister, are you heartless? *Look at me!*"

Omakayas turned to look at Pinch and, perhaps heart-lessly but certainly helplessly, laughed. There he stood, his hair every which way, full of leaves, and gaag quills across his shoulders and down one arm. There were quills in his cheeks and even one sticking from the end of his nose.

"Ahhh, ahhhh," Omakayas could not contain herself. The laughter overwhelmed her. She fell on the ground, then had to force herself up, saying, "Brother, I pity you, but you look . . . ahhhh, ahhhh." The quill on the end of his nose undid her and she fell down laughing again.

"Hiyn, brother, I am sorry for you. Let me help."

Pinch was savagely pulling the quills out with his own fingers, screaming with every one. In his pain, he grabbed the quills so carelessly that they stuck his hands. Now his fingers were also quilled.

"Oh, Quillboy, my brother, let me help you. Please, be still."

But first, Omakayas lifted her knife yet another time to deal with the little porcupine, which was trying to sneak away. To her surprise, Pinch, or Quill, as he'd be known once this story was told, said, "No, leave it."

"Gaawiin, I'm hungry!" said Omakayas.

"Me too, but I'll catch something else," said Pinch.

"What do you mean?"

"A warrior does not take revenge on the helpless," said Pinch solemnly. "I shall spare its life."

"Well, I'll leave it for now," said Omakayas, eyeing the juicy creature, "but once you suffer the removal of these quills you may decide to revenge yourself. This porcupine wasn't all that helpless."

Pinch let his sister pluck out the quills with careful fingers, making a noise as each one came out.

"Ow! Wah! Ow-wahee-*oooh*!"

Omakayas put each quill on a piece of bark until she had a little stack, and when she was finished she meticulously wrapped the quills in the bark and put them in the pouch at her waist.

By now the porcupine was watching them curiously, no longer interested in leaving. Quill plucked a little soft bark from the base of a green stick and gave it to the trusting creature. It made a happy little clucking sound and began to munch.

"Perhaps," he said in a portentous voice, "this will be my medicine animal."

"I will make you something with these quills, to honor your great battle with the gaag," said Omakayas.

"Ahhh, sister, you do me too much honor," said Quillboy. "Way too much. I wish you'd just forget about the battle, but let's keep this little gaag."

"Alas, I can't forget," said Omakayas. "The memory of your fierce display is burned into my heart!" It was bad of her, but she still wanted to laugh. Now poor Quillboy was pocked with little holes all over his arm and shoulders. The hole in his nose made him even more ridiculous.

"You look like you were in a battle with a thousand miniature warriors. And they hit you with their arrows. Tiny ones." Omakayas twisted her face to stop her laughter, but a snort escaped. She pretended to control herself. "My brother, I am in awe of the great deed you did today!"

"Then I'm making a fire," said Pinch. "Give me your striker. If our enemies discover us, I'll quill them to death. I am not Quillboy, but Quill. Just Quill. The great Quill! We're going to feast on my courage now."

Omakayas turned, though she didn't much feel like killing the little porcupine. She lifted her knife one last time.

"No! Don't kill my porcupine! I'll find some other food!"

Pinch strode out into the lake until the water was thigh-deep. Omakayas was exasperated with her brother's odd behavior and was now even hungrier. Pinch stood dramatically in the shallows and said, "Look!"

He plunged his hand down and, to his shock, came up with a fish.

"What?" he said, gaping at the fish in his hand. He ran to shore. "How? Look, sister! The porcupine is definitely a helping spirit!"

Omakayas looked down at the little porcupine. It gazed shyly up at her. It blinked. You really can't pet a porcupine, thought Omakayas. What would Quill do with it?

Quill threw the fish at Omakayas's feet with an annoying grunt, just like the grown-up warriors sometimes did when they killed a moose or a massive beaver.

"It's not that *big* a fish, Quillboy," said Omakayas.

"Did *you* ever catch a fish with your bare hands?"

"No," said Omakayas. She banged the fish against a rock and proceeded to clean it with swift expertise.

"I didn't think so," said Quill.

After they had roasted the fish and eaten it, Quill reached out and grasped the porcupine's front paws and swung the little creature onto his head. The porcupine dug its dull claws into the mass of knotted Quillboy hair, and soon, to Omakayas's amazement, it went to sleep.

THREE

THE MEMEGWESI

As soon as they'd eaten, the two set out with full stomachs and new energy. They hoisted the canoe, turned it over, and set it on their shoulders. The porcupine, amazingly, balanced easily on Quill's head. Its tail hung down Quill's neck, but the quills couldn't pierce his thick hair. Quill had made cushions of moss to place upon their shoulders where the canoe rested heaviest, and as they walked along Omakayas felt fine. This wouldn't be so bad. Easy enough, maybe, if they stuck to the older parts of the forest along the river, where there was less undergrowth to tangle them up.

Quill and Omakayas walked all morning. The sun was

just overhead when they heard the roar of the rapids they had traversed the night before. Curious, they set the canoe down in the woods. Omakayas saw that the porcupine was still stuck to her brother's head. She was now getting used to it.

"That porcupine looks better than your usual hairdo," she said.

Quill just nodded, as if she'd given him a compliment. The porcupine held on.

"Sister, let's go see where we were in that rapids," said Quill. "I'm starting to forget already."

"It went so fast," Omakayas agreed. "Like a dream. I can't remember much about it either."

As they walked toward the sound of the water, their words were soon drowned out by the noise. Getting closer, they began to feel a little puffed out over, then more than proud of, what they'd come through. They even turned and grinned at each other, nodding as if to say, We're river warriors! Ahau! They felt this excitement up until the moment they broke through the underbrush and saw the river.

Their mouths fell open. They forgot to breathe, forgot to swallow. And they knew. It wasn't them. It could not have been them or any expertise they had. Nobody could have made it out of what they saw, not alive. A ragged and ever changing wall of water twisting with power surged out at them. It was uncanny, killing, and a terrible marvel all at once. In its mouth, there was no possibility of any life surviving. None at all. Yet here they were. Saved by the spirits, Manidoog, kept safe by the Gizhe Manidoo, the greatest and kindest one, or perhaps by the whim of the chill Manidoog who lived in the stones.

Whatever had saved them was beyond and greater than any human strength or skill. They saw this at once and stood mute at the sight.

As they stood there, a small figure rose on the opposite bank. To both of them, it looked at first like a small child with a hairy head. They crouched low. The little person moved his arm, as if making an offering to the rapids, and they saw that he was proportioned like a fully grown Anishinabe man. He was dressed in buckskins and knee-high makizinan, and his hair stuck out all over, like Quill's

hair. At the sight, Quill put his hand up to his head, thinking exactly that thought. *You're like me.* Luckily, he remembered not to touch the porcupine. Then the little person stepped backward and was gone. Just like that.

Omakayas and Quill looked at each other, wide-eyed. They mouthed the word *memegwesi* together, then nodded and smiled and looked back at the raging water. He was, perhaps, the spirit who had helped them through. Omakayas had only one thing that she could give—the red beads around her neck, the ones from her grandmother, Nokomis. They were hard to relinquish. But slowly, she took them off, crept as close to the river as she dared, and placed them on a rock where the memegwesi would surely find them once they left. Only after they'd turned away, and got back on their path, did she remember how the beads had appeared in her morning dream.

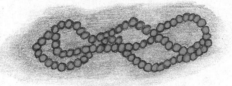

JIIBAYAG

The day went on and on. They got lost, and they stumbled this way and that, beneath the canoe. Finally Omakayas agreed to hide the canoe safely in the woods. She decided that they could find their camp more easily if they walked to the river, doubled back, and eased their way along the shore. They were on the same side of the river as their camp, but somehow, in trying to find easier ways to carry the canoe, they'd gone past their family. And now it was beginning to grow dark. Soon night would fall and they'd have to spend it on the cold ground. Suddenly, they realized where they were. Camp was just ahead! Eagerly, Omakayas and Quill made their way through the bush. But they stopped short, hearing from their camp the awful cries and wails, the unmistakable sounds of disaster and of mourning.

Chilled, they grabbed each other's arms.

Someone had died in the time they'd been gone—both of their hearts skipped. They froze. Who could it have been? Was it Nokomis—old and vulnerable? Surely not Mama, or Deydey, and not Old Tallow, who was tough as leather and unkillable. Not one of them. But there was their beautiful older sister, Angeline, who'd barely survived smallpox, and Fishtail, her husband, who'd nearly died back then, too. Omakayas shook now, shuddered, for she had already lost her baby brother to that terrible visitor. She did not want to climb the mountain of grief again. Animikiins, Little Thunder, and his father were also traveling with them—perhaps an accident had occurred. And there was the tiniest one, Bizheens, the little lynx with his watching eyes. He was a quiet and clever baby boy just learning to speak and even more devoted to Omakayas than to Mama.

Dagasana, nimishoomis, Gizhe Manidoo, Omakayas closed her eyes and prayed. She knew that she could not survive the loss of a little brother, not again. But the truth was she didn't think that she could survive the loss of anyone.

And Quill clearly felt the same. Tears trembled in his eyes.

"Let's sneak up on them," he whispered to her, "and find out who it was before we enter camp. I can't bear it. I'm afraid my heart will burst out of my chest!"

"Mine hurts too, already. I'm so afraid, brother, just like you."

And so the two crept close and hid in the bushes just outside the camp, fearful as mice, wary and timid as rabbits, horrified. Lumps in their throats, hearts beating painfully, they listened as Nokomis raised her hands in the air and spoke. From where they were, they could tell that Nokomis was still breathing quickly, as if she had run through the woods. Her back was turned from them. But she was definitely alive. Omakayas was glad she could not see her beloved grandmother's grieving face.

"When I found these on the rocks, I knew what had happened," she cried, holding something out to show the rest of the family. There was a beat of silence, and then a wild cry. It was a strangled scream, a high-pitched bleat, and it came from the tough old woman who had once saved Omakayas's life—Old Tallow.

"Gaawiin, it cannot be!" Mama's voice—then pande-
monium. It was impossible to tell who was there and who
was not. The yells of sorrow were all mixed up into one
barking wail.

"I can't tell who died," Omakayas was crying hard now.
"I don't know what to do."

"I know!" whispered Quill.

"What?"

"It's us!"

"Us?"

"Nokomis holds your red beads out, I see it now. She
found them on the rock. *It's us that were killed.*"

"Let's go." Omakayas's heart lifted with happiness and
she strained forward, but Quill grabbed her arm.

"No! Wait!"

Unbelieving, Omakayas shook away from her brother.
He looked crazy with the porcupine on his head, and he
was actually grinning. With a sinking heart she knew that
he had an idea, one that would surely get them in trouble.

"There will *never* be a chance like this one!"

"No!" Omakayas shook his arm, then punched him.
She knew him well. What mischief was in his mind! It all
happened so quickly—he could go from inconsolable
sorrow to plotting a joke in one instant. Somehow, he
could make her forget that her family's hearts were breaking just beyond the fringe of bushes. He could make her
curious about what he was thinking.

"I'll be right back!" said Quill. "It's just the right time of evening to scare them. I'm going to sneak my hand into Mama's pack and take a couple of handfuls of her white flour. We'll powder ourselves up and walk back into the camp as ghosts, as jiibayag!"

"No!"

"Yes! They'll talk about this joke so much we will be famous! Oh, they'll never forget!"

In spite of herself, and even knowing how stricken her family was, Omakayas did something that she would regret for many years to come. She let herself be persuaded.

"I don't know. Wewiib! Hurry up before I change my mind!"

Quill was gone and back so quickly that she hardly had time to think.

"This is wrong," she mumbled as Quill smoothed the flour on her face and arms.

"But *very* funny," said Quill, patting the flour onto himself, turning his cheeks white, then throwing some flour up onto the porcupine, which licked its little mouth in appreciation.

"We look like chimookomanag."

"Except white people don't wear porcupines on their heads. Okay. Let's go."

As she stepped into the camp behind her brother, Omakayas knew that this was a very bad idea, and yet, something in her was thrilled. It was the *chance* of the situation. The opportunity for a wild joke, just given to them!

The two walked into camp.

Quill stood with a strange, vacant, dead-spirit expression. The porcupine's quills went up. Its eyes gleamed in the white flour. Quill moaned a little, and waited until he was noticed. Omakayas stood with him, immediately stricken when she saw that they'd succeeded in horrifying their family beyond Quill's wildest hopes.

Bizheens howled. Mama cried out. Deydey's eyes flew wide open. Nokomis dropped to the earth with her hand on her chest. Angeline grabbed Fishtail. Animikiins and his father, Miskobines, stood stock-still, mouths gaping.

But Old Tallow never missed a beat. She sicced her dogs on them.

The dogs wouldn't attack Omakayas, whom they loved. They knew Old Tallow had a special place in her heart for the girl. But they jumped on Quill and knocked him flat, then went off howling when the porcupine swatted them with its tail. As soon as everyone realized Quill was a real boy, not a ghost, Mama ran up and slapped him on the head and hugged him at the same time. Deydey narrowed his eyes and scowled. Angeline furiously turned away and went back into the wigwam. Fishtail, Animikiins, and Miskobines all grinned with admiration.

"How did you get that porcupine to stay on your head?" asked Animikiins.

Nokomis threw tobacco in the fire to appease the real spirits of the dead, to thank the Manidoog for returning the children, and because she didn't know what else to do. Old Tallow sat motionless with a combination of disgust and relief on her face. Only little Bizheens ran up to Omakayas and hugged her.

"Giizhawenimin. Giizhawenimin," he said. "I really love you."

And Omakayas began to cry, as much ashamed of herself now as she was glad to be back, alive. Nokomis was the first to laugh. It was a tentative little snort, muffled with her hand, and she had tears in her eyes, too, so the laugh was half reproachful. But that laugh was enough for Fishtail, who let out a honk of amusement. Soon everyone in camp was either crying or laughing, and although Mama continued to pretend to strike her son he only ducked under her mock blows until she fell over, laughing too, in great relief.

The little porcupine looked up dreamily at them all and kept licking the flour from its paws. Omakayas grew dizzy with laughter and sat on the ground, holding Bizheens, who was always ready to coo and clap when he saw people happy. His sharp, lively eyes shone in the camp light, and he threw his arms again and again around Omakayas. He was the best thing that had ever happened to her, *ever*, she thought, this little brother who adored her no matter what she did.

Not long and the family was eating, dunking bannock in venison soup, talking, rehashing all that had happened to Omakayas and Quill. The porcupine was back on Quill's head, in its accustomed spot. It was beginning to smell a little funny, and Mama said that Quill would have to sleep outside with it or wash.

"I will choose to live with my medicine," said Quill. "Even though my family shuns me!"

Everyone agreed that Quill was the perfect name for him from then on. Omakayas told about the lake at the end of the rapids, about its sandy, empty shores, and it was agreed that the family would break their camp and portage to that same lake. It sounded like the perfect place to set up camp and collect supplies of dried fish, meat, and berries so they could continue their journey.

FOUR

BEARS AND HEART BERRIES

O n the other side of the lake with the golden, sandy shores, there was a broad patch of sunlit meadow, an opening in the dense pine forest. The grass was filled with juicy wild strawberries called ode'iminan, heart berries. All of the plants were either in bloom or bearing dewy fruit. Two thin, scruffy black bears were lapping and scraping the berries into their mouths, heads swinging in the morning grass. Suddenly they looked up, reared back on strong haunches, peered forward with their weak little eyes, and sniffed the breeze with their sensitive, all-seeing noses. *Ah,* they seemed to say, huffing and chuttering deep in their throats, *it is those unpredictable ones, those creatures*

who sometimes fear us and sometimes kill us! After a moment of hesitation, not wanting to leave before their bellies were bursting, they groaned, jumped away, and hid themselves in the woods.

They watched from behind the trees. Their noses twitched to catch information about the humans.

When Omakayas came into the field, she knew that the bears had been there first. There were the tracks, the scattered droppings, the raked-up plants, and even the faint, rotten, yet somehow comforting odor of bear. She gestured to Mama, Nokomis, and Bizheens.

"Over here, ambe! There's lots and lots of berries!"

The rest of the family came after her. Bizheens was now walking comically along on fat bowlegs. He carried a tiny makak made out of birchbark, a gathering basket that Omakayas had made especially for him. He could not remember berries from the year before, they were new to him all over again, so Omakayas carefully showed him how to pluck a berry with his chubby fingers and pop it into his mouth. His eyes widened with joy.

"Minopogwad ina? Does it taste good?"

Bizheens's silky curls bobbed up and down. Just like Omakayas, he'd been adopted into the family. The two were taken in by the bighearted mother of them all, Yellow Kettle, and by Nokomis. Nobody knew where the toddler's curly hair came from, but Mama was proud of its shine and beauty. She ruffled Bizheens's hair and arranged it every morning. Deydey teased her, saying she'd spoil Bizheens, but she waved away his words and pointed at the empty black kettle. He'd best go out and find something to fill it!

Deydey and Old Tallow hunted for their meat, as did Animikiins and the old chief, Miskobines. Quill even brought back a partridge or trapped a fish from time to time. But though they could hunt, too, and set snares every morning, the women loved gathering the new fruits and berries of the spring. They could spend hours picking, eating enough berries to keep their strength up, of course, and filling their makakoon.

Now as they bent to their work in the sun of the new summer, the women talked. Omakayas told her grandmother, once again, about the little person she had seen at the rapids. Another memegwesi had once helped Nokomis when she was lost, long ago, when she was very young. These helping people, small and sometimes hairy, were friendly to the Anishinabeg and it was a special honor to see one. Grown people rarely did. The memegwesiwag usually showed themselves to children.

"Why is that?" Omakayas asked her grandmother.

"Children have open eyes, and open hearts. They see things that we cannot. Look at Bizheens."

Her little brother was staring across the meadow of strawberries, past Mama, at something in the woods. Every so often he would stare into the leaves, then go back to eating the berries that he carefully picked from the low plants.

"Does he have a single berry in his makak yet?"

"No," said Omakayas, laughing.

She put a few of her own berries in his gathering basket, and he smiled at her, plucked them out, and ate them, too.

"He sees something," Mama said.

Although she was bent low to the earth, picking with great speed and industry, she had noticed that her baby was watching something. Omakayas always marveled at this quality in her mother. She would seem absorbed by some task—say, cooking or sewing—and yet she could immediately tell when Omakayas was taking a break from tanning a hide, or when Quill was cooking up some mischief in his brain. She would bark at Omakayas—*Get back to it!* Or at Quill—*Put your mind on something useful!* It was as though Mama had an invisible hat made of eyes that noticed everything on all sides of her head. Nobody got away with anything around Yellow Kettle.

"Maybe he's watching a little bird," said Mama. "A little gijigijigaaneshiinh. I hear one calling."

Omakayas heard the gijigijigaaneshiinh, too. The tiny bird with the black cap sang, *Shii-me, shii-me.*

"Looking for its little sister," said Nokomis. Last winter, she had told a story about how those little birds had once been boys who lost their little sister in the woods. Omakayas wanted to ask for the story again but knew that Nokomis would only tell her to wait until the snakes and frogs were sleeping. The Ojibwe told stories only in the winter.

Shii-me, shii-me, sang the birds, hopping from branch to branch.

They were singing *at* something, thought Omakayas, standing up suddenly. They were calling out a warning, perhaps, or just scolding at something in the woods with them. Birds are always giving notice of intruders. It is hard to hide in the woods when wings have such watchful eyes. Omakayas took a step after Bizheens, who had toddled toward some particularly juicy berries, and then she saw the bears, as they materialized suddenly from the light shield of leaves.

When bears are still restoring their lost winter fat, they can be dangerously hungry. They usually respect humans.

But a small human, a little fat one like the boy tumbling toward them, might be tempting. The two bears had lingered, hungry for berries, their stomachs aching. The longer they waited to get back to the berries, the more their bellies hurt. And then that juicy little animal came ambling right toward them. A treat! They were just deciding whether to jump forward and grab the tender young creature and speed away, when another human was suddenly before them. This one was bigger, unafraid, and definitely more difficult to deal with. It made an awful noise. A surprising noise.

"Gego! Gego! Gego!"

Omakayas ran forward and jumped in front of Bizheens.

"Saa, shame on you bears! He's my little brother!"

Omakayas held Bizheens back with her legs and waved her arms at the bears to make herself bigger. She let them know they wouldn't get to the sweet little morsel behind her so easily.

"Majaan!" She shouted at them to shoo, to get out of the way. Mama ran up too and began to bang on her pail. Nokomis yelled as loudly as she could. Bizheens began to whimper, surprised and frightened at the commotion. Then he screamed, and his scream was as loud as his namesake's, the lynx's, or even a bigger cat, the cougar. That did it! The startled bears stepped backward and then panicked, tumbled over each other, whirling to get away from these furious beings who had just moments before seemed so calm and vulnerable.

Omakayas had to laugh—they looked almost embarrassed by what had happened. She had been close to bears many times, and although she respected them, she was somehow not afraid of them. That was because when she was very little she had had a dream in which bears were her protectors.

"There they go," said Nokomis, fanning the heat from her face.

Scooped into Mama's arms, Bizheens stopped crying and began to play with her bead necklaces. After this, although the three women continued to pick, they kept themselves in a circle around Bizheens. At last, his belly tight, his mouth, cheeks, and face red with berry juice, he tumbled over and slept. Mama hoisted him onto her back and tied him to her with a cloth. Now he would be safe.

Nokomis sighed, looking at him.

"There was a girl who was a bear, once, in the old times," she said.

"Really?" said Omakayas, and in spite of herself she asked for the story.

"I can't tell you about it until the frogs and snakes are sleeping," said Nokomis, predictably. "Don't forget to ask me once the snow falls."

Omakayas stood up, grumpily wishing for that story. But she knew that if underground and underwater creatures heard the stories, they might repeat them to the powerful underwater spirits, or the great spirits of the animals, who might be angry at the Ojibwe for talking about them. But her disappointment melted at the sight of her little brother's rosy, stained face. She loved him so dearly and she'd never let the bears steal him away!

They were soon done, except for a patch by the place they had seen the bears.

"We should leave them some," said Nokomis.

"After all," said Omakayas, "they didn't bother us much."

"Huh, what we left them is hardly a mouthful to a bear," said Mama.

"Still, they'll know we thought of them," said Omakayas, staring thoughtfully at the place the bears had vanished.

WORKING HIDES

When they returned to the camp on the shores of the wide, calm lake, Mama added some of the berries to the stew that she was making and spread the others out to dry on a big piece of birchbark. She sat down near the berries to work on reed mats for the floor of their wigwam, and to shoo away birds. Nokomis had one hide draped over a log and she was working on it with a thick piece of wood. Using a sharpened deer's horn, Omakayas began to help her sister, Angeline, scrape and work a deer hide stretched out between two trees. She sighed deeply. When the family had left the island, she'd also left the special scraper that her father had made for her out of an old gun barrel. Perhaps she'd imagined that she'd get out of the constant hide-scraping. No such luck! Now she wished she had the old scraper, which was better. It was boring work, and stinky too. But doing chores with Angeline was not  so bad anymore, because ever since they'd left home, they'd been homesick together. As they worked, they often spoke of their island.

"Remember that funny old trader, his big belly?" asked Omakayas.

"You are still wearing the dress we bought from him with that dried fish!"

"And the chimookoman girl, the Break-Apart Girl— do you think she's taking good care of my dog?"

"She is feeding him her own food," said Angeline kindly. "I'm sure she's being good to him."

"I hope so," said Omakayas. "Do you ever think of the school you went to?"

39

"I practice the chimookomanag writing," said Angeline. "I keep trying to teach Fishtail, but his hands are big and clumsy! Do you want a lesson?"

Whenever Angeline was in the mood to teach, Omakayas always took the chance to learn from her. Angeline had written the chimookoman alphabet on a piece of birchbark. Omakayas had tried to impress her sister by memorizing it. When they took a break from working on the hides, Angeline helped Omakayas with the letters.

"Your *S* letters look better than mine," said Angeline. That was all it took for Omakayas to try even harder to follow and remember the squiggles and dots that held meaning.

Later, they put the birchbark down and went back to working the hides. They moved together, talking of Nokomis's garden back on the island, and of Omakayas's pet crow, Andeg. Shadows lengthened, the light deepened, and soon there was the crackling sound of the hunters coming through the brush—two of them at least, Animikiins and his father. The old man appeared first, and Animikiins came after him, carrying a couple of fat rabbits. Though the two had gone out with the hope of killing something bigger, the snares set close to camp had paid off.

"It's not a bear, but at least we have something," said Animikiins.

Omakayas smiled at him—he never teased her the way Quill did. He was taught to be careful and respectful, and he tried to listen to his elders. She could see it. But Animikiins also had an explosive temper, like Mama's, and he was easily hurt or shamed. He could not always contain his feelings. He scowled and glared if he thought he was being teased. Omakayas was always careful around him, and she didn't talk very much.

"Miigwech," she simply said now. She didn't dare say much else, for one never knew. Animikiins might take offense.

"Huh."

That was his answer. He nodded his head abruptly and turned away. But there was something in the way he'd

looked at her, almost with admiration, that made Omakayas feel unexpectedly warm. A soft, tingling blush rose and crept around her face.

Later, Omakayas skinned the rabbits with a few slices of her knife, and with a few quick jerks she peeled off their fur.

"You do that well," said Nokomis.

Her praise was sweet, and Omakayas smiled. The night was warm, and after eating everyone slept outside, around the campfire. The first mosquitoes had hatched, but the smoke from the fire confused the zagimeg. They couldn't torment the family with their fierce, annoying whines and stings. As Omakayas drowsed, she heard Quill and the porcupine, just beyond the circle of the campfire. The little porcupine breathed quickly, in light panting gusts, and made soft chirrups in its sleep, as if it was dreaming a delightful dream. Omakayas stayed awake just to listen to the comical and charming way it breathed and even lightly snored, but then her attention was caught by talk from the grown-ups.

GOING NORTH

They were not laughing at old times, as they did so often, or reviewing the day in low voices, either. After leaving the island, they had stayed close by the great lake, unwilling to leave it entirely. But the two winters had been very difficult. Now the family wanted to find land where they could settle. They had expected to meet up with relatives, but had missed them.

"We should continue north, giiwedin," said Old Tallow. "Few chimookomanag have made their homes in the great woods and lakes. We don't want them to kick us out again!"

"I still think that my brother might come through this way," said Deydey. "This is our old stomping ground. We hunted here long ago. But now . . ."

"Game is getting scarce."

"There is always good fishing on this lake. But I think we are camped close to the big path of our enemies, the Bwaanag. If their warriors come across us on their way back to their homes, after a raid—mad that they got nothing, howah!—we'd be in big trouble!"

"At least we know where my aunt Muskrat is," said Angeline. "We can't miss if we have to move on, north. We'll end up at her camp."

"*Without* her annoying husband, I hope," said Mama. Yellow Kettle had never liked Albert LaPautre, and believed that he tended to drink the ishkodewaaboo, the white man's water that sent people out of their minds.

"Both Muskrat's and Fishtail's people live up there now. We could stay with them. They're all relatives. I miss those little girls, too."

"Two Strike probably rules the islands by now," laughed Nokomis, remembering Two Strike's imperious ways and ferocious scowl when crossed.

"She'll be surprised to see my dogs," growled Old Tallow. "She'd best beware! My dogs have endless memories! They will never forget how that girl made war against them. They know as much as, or even more than, humans. Their ancestors speak to them in their dreams and tell them which humans to trust. They trust my Omakayas, who is always kind to them."

Omakayas warmed to the rough approval from Old Tallow.

It seemed long ago that Omakayas's cousin Two Strike Girl had made war on Old Tallow's dogs and ended up receiving a thrashing from the fierce old woman. Deydey laughed, remembering how poor Pinch had gotten out of that jam—caught between his duty as a warrior answering to Two Strike, and his loyalty to Old Tallow and her dog tribe.

"I want to plant my garden," said Nokomis. "The seeds in my bark packs are longing to be set in the earth and sprout!"

"We need those northern berry patches," said Miskobines. "An old man gets a longing for berries."

"An old man needs his sweets, for sure," teased Nokomis. "I think you want to see Auntie Muskrat because your tooth hurts for sugar!"

"Aiigh!" Miskobines swiped at Nokomis, but it was true that he had admired the round and capable Muskrat and praised her cooking to the skies. He'd made no secret of his disappointment when Muskrat's husband had returned.

"We need wild rice beds, for sure," Yellow Kettle insisted. "We can't depend on these men to get lucky hunting all next winter. We don't want to starve. We'll have to make a cache to keep us going this year."

Miskobines reminded them that at their last stop, Sandy Lake, they'd heard that the government had a plan for the Anishinabeg.

"There is talk of making one big home for all of us, over near the land of the Bwaan, where we get the white clay."

Deydey did not trust the white people, the chimooko-manag. He did not trust the chiefs. He did not trust the one they called "great father" off in Washington. *He is not my great father*, Deydey would say. *I have seen him starve our people. I have seen him take our land. No father kills his children and leaves them homeless!* So Deydey did not trust the idea of one big homeland for all of the Anishinabeg.

"That place where they get the white clay is beautiful," said Old Tallow, "but once we are there will the agents keep their promises?"

"No home would be big enough. We do things very differently, even though we speak the same language," said Nokomis.

"There could be fighting," Miskobines agreed.

"And not enough food," said Yellow Kettle.

"Yes, we should go north, way north, giiwedin, to where my Muskrat lives," said Nokomis. "We should live near Muskrat."

Omakayas's heart jumped. Her Auntie Muskrat had traveled north to the big lake, the one with the many islands. The French called that place Lac du Bois, but the people there had many names for its bays and points and narrows. Omakayas wanted to go there, too; her favorite playmates were there—her cousins Twilight, Little Bee or Amoosens, and even Two Strike. She missed them awfully, and the thought of going to live with them was so wonderful to her that she shouted out loud from her blankets.

"Geget, izhaadah! Let's go!"

"Was that a ghost?"

Deydey's rough voice hushed her up. But as she fell asleep she smiled at the thought of seeing her beloved cousins.

Omakayas woke to the delicate patting of tiny paws on her face. Quill's porcupine was curious and hungry, but gentle. He tugged on the end of her nose, as if wondering whether it was permanently attached. His hard, wet,

little nose burrowed under her hair, along her neck. At last, he stuck his nose in her ear and snuffled. That got results. Omakayas turned over and shrugged him off, careful to avoid his quills. Frowning, she surfaced out of a dream. She had dreamed of her cousin Two Strike Girl. As usual, Two Strike was taunting her. Two Strike held a huge fish she'd caught, a beautiful silver-white fish. The fish turned to Omakayas and cried, "Guess who caught me? Hah, hah, hah! You'll never be as powerful as Two Strike!"

This was not a dream that Omakayas wanted to continue, anyway. She rolled out of her blanket and laughed when the porcupine tumbled at her feet and groaned softly as it righted itself. In spite of her dream, Omakayas hoped that the elders had decided to travel north toward the vast islanded lake where her cousins lived. No matter how hard it might be to live in the shadow of her strong cousin, Two Strike, she missed them all. Omakayas could almost smell the fish stew her Auntie Muskrat might be cooking. Soon, oh how soon, they would all be together, just the way they had been back in the golden days on the golden island, when she was small.

FIVE

PRAYER FEATHERS

Today, Deydey had a job for her and Omakayas was relieved to hear that it was not tanning hides. He asked her to make his favorite traveling food—venison pounded dry with berries and covered with boiled fat. This food could be carried in hide pouches, over great distances, and it always tasted good when boiled with whatever could be found to add. A deer carcass, which Deydey had brought to the camp the day before, had hung the night in a tree. Now Nokomis helped lower it and they took it out onto the shore.

"Cut it thin," said Nokomis. The meat would dry on the racks constructed of long birch sticks. Their knives, bought from the trader back on Madeline Island, were very sharp, and each tender strip was sliced very thin to dry quickly. As for the berries, Old Tallow and Angeline were collecting more to add to the ones they had gathered. The day was hot, and already the berries from the day before were puckering nicely. If only the little porcupine could leave them alone! Every time Omakayas turned her back, he tried to waddle over to the berries and began delicately but quickly plucking them up and shoving them into his mouth with his black paws. He was like a naughty little boy, but very slow, and always when he turned to look up at her he seemed so sleepy and bewildered that she had to laugh.

"I see that Quill has left his medicine animal to me," said Omakayas, shooing him off. She brought an armful of fresh, sweet willow over and the porcupine dug into it like a little man into a feast. The sun grew hot overhead. Omakayas built a slow fire out of cedar sticks just where the smoke would flavor the meat. Then she retreated into a leafy strip of shade beside the beach.

Soon the porcupine came toward her with his belly dragging, comical and huge. He groaned with satisfaction and curled on the ground close enough for her to smell him. She edged a bit away, wondering if she smelled as bad to him as he did to her. He sighed a little and closed his eyes. There was something about the porcupine's happy sleep that made Omakayas sleepy too. Even though it wasn't even the middle of the day yet, her eyes closed. The sound of lapping waves soothed her and she relaxed deep into the sand. There was a shadow, a swooping shadow. Her eyes opened. Nothing. She glanced over at the rack of meat and then jumped up, tumbling the porcupine into a tangle of tree roots. Gone! The strips of meat! Many of them were gone! And yet the seagulls hadn't discovered the rack. She would have heard them. They never kept quiet. No, she suspected quite another culprit. But one that she could put to her own use. An eagle.

She'd once heard Old Tallow and her Deydey speak of catching an eagle by putting fish out on a rack and crouching beneath. It had taken them a very long time to attract the bird, but Omakayas had a chance right then. For an eagle had already discovered the dried meat and would return for more. A feather plucked from a living eagle was much more powerful than a feather that an eagle has dropped—the feather still had life in it. The eagle was still flying to the creator, bearing prayers on the wind.

Carefully, she crept over to the rack of sticks and put one of the extra pieces of birchbark over her head and shoulders. She poked holes in two slabs of the deer meat and used more of the twining root to secure the meat to her wrists with long cords. She draped the meat on the topmost rung of the drying rack. Then she crouched underneath the birchbark, in the broiling sun, to wait.

The wait seemed endless. She saw through a strip torn

in the bark. Clear sky. A cloud or two. The waves rolled gently up the shore and withdrew with a hissing sound that made her sleepy again. All of a sudden, she sensed the shadow before the bird, felt the sudden yank on her wrists as the meat was plucked from the rack. The eagle's shock rang through her arms as she jumped up and clutched its tail with both hands. The eagle screamed and struck at her face with the cruel hook of its razor-sharp beak—but she felt nothing. The great bird let go of the meat and soared off and Omakayas stood still, upright, the meat rack collapsed at her feet. In each hand, she clutched two pure white eagle feathers. Feathers that had never touched the ground. Omakayas brought the feathers to her forehead and found that she was weeping.

"N'dawnis! N'dawnis!" It was Deydey shouting. He had come out of the woods just in time to see his daughter hanging fiercely on to the tail of an eagle. He rushed to her and touched the side of her face. Her Deydey was big and forbidding, and never seemed to like to be around other people. But he could also be childish in his laughter and delight. Or, as now, he could be very tender. He pressed the edge of his tough thumb on Omakayas's cheek, where the eagle had ripped at her with its beak.

"N'dawnis, why did you do that?" he asked.

"Deydey, I heard you say once that to take the feathers from the sky was good, that they should never touch the ground."

"You have done something, n'dawnis," said Deydey, "that a warrior does. This is something that only grown men do. And you are just a little girl."

Ashamed of her tears, Omakayas raised her hands to her face. Deydey took the eagle feathers from her hands. He brushed the tears from her eyes with the tips of the white feathers.

"N'dawnis, you are no longer a child. You have the courage to call down an eagle, and you have taken these feathers. We must have a feast for you and for that grandfather, that eagle, and perhaps you will receive a new name, my girl. Your name Omakayas, Little Frog, was the nickname that we gave you when your first step reminded us of the hopping of a little frog."

"Deydey, please, dagasana," said Omakayas as her father carefully put the white feathers in his shirt, against his breast, "I don't want another name. I want to keep my baby name, my nickname. I am Omakayas."

Deydey smiled at her and stroked her hair.

"That is a humble thing to say, my girl. And a brave thing you did. You make me proud," he said.

In the shade, there was a snorting as the porcupine woke and settled back into munching fresh willow.

As she helped build the rack back up and replace the slices of meat on it, and as she washed sand off the pieces that had fallen onto the ground, Omakayas felt something balloon up inside of her like a cloud. It was a strange, buoyant feeling—she felt that she could be lifted away by it. As if she'd held on to an eagle and been dragged up into the air! After Deydey left, she understood what it was—pride. It was so rare that Deydey ever showed that he was proud of what she'd done.

That evening, Deydey smoked his pipe and thought about what to do with the eagle feathers. The next day he talked to the family and said that they would have to build a sweat lodge right there. He had dreamed of a name for Omakayas and had to give it to her right away. So the sweat lodge was built. Fishtail cut pliable green willow and he and Animikiins bent the poles and anchored them in the ground. Angeline and Quill laced the poles together. Nokomis and Omakayas gathered the skins and blankets that they would drape over the sweat lodge to keep in the heat. Old Tallow hunted out the strongest grandfathers, the asiniig, the stones that would be heated white-hot and then carried into the fire pit in the center of the lodge. When medicines were placed on these rocks and water splashed over them, the steam would rise. First the women would use the lodge, then the men. There would be two separate ceremonies that night.

Yellow Kettle was excited all day and worked on special feast dishes. She made a venison stew. She dug and softened roots for little cakes to fry in the grease of a huge beaver tail. Several times, she looked longingly at Quill's porcupine.

"My mother! Take your mind away!" Quill was shocked at her idea, which he could see clearly in her eyes. "Don't think of making my little friend into soup," he cried.

When everything was ready at last, the women went into the sweat lodge. Old Tallow and Nokomis sat by the door, and Yellow Kettle sat to the north. Angeline and Omakayas sat close together in the south. The heated rocks were lifted in with the deer antlers, and Nokomis placed pinches of fragrant medicines on the rocks. Then the door was closed. There was utter darkness. Old Tallow splashed a ladle full of water on the rocks and the steam surrounded them, warm and cozy at first, then hot. Nokomis uttered prayers and the steam got even hotter. On Omakayas's cheek, the wound from the eagle burned and ached. And then Old Tallow prayed and the steam became unbearable. Omakayas was determined not to put her head down to the place behind her where the skins met the earth. There, she could lift the edge of the skin and snatch a cool breath. She managed not to, but she had to lie down when she got dizzy. At last, when the door was opened and the women crawled out, it was the men's turn. Old Tallow would keep the fire and bring the rocks.

Outside, sitting in the cool air of the night, drinking gulps of pure water, Omakayas felt deliciously calm and happy. The sweat lodge always made her feel good— afterward. She listened to the songs and prayers of the men and heard the calling of the night birds, the thrum of crickets, the whisper of the pines. Deydey lifted the blanket covering the door to the lodge and called her over to him. Omakayas came and knelt in the entrance.

"In my dream a bird appeared, great and white, and in its beak it carried these feathers." Deydey fanned her with the feathers she had plucked from the eagle. "I heard my grandmother calling and then I saw her—but she was not old, as I remembered, but a young girl." Deydey gave the feathers to Omakayas to hold and touched her cheek where the eagle had raked her. Most of the wound would heal, but she would have a tiny scar. He dabbed her wound with warm bear grease and put his hands on her head. He smoothed her hair with a powerful, gentle touch. Then his hands rested on her cheeks and he looked kindly into her face.

"Your name is Ogimabinesikwe," he said. "That was my grandmother's name, and it is your name now. The spirits will know you by this name. Leading Thunderbird Woman. You can still let us call you Omakayas if you want, but the spirits will know you by this other name, too."

"It is a good name," said Old Tallow, delighted. She laughed out loud with rare excitement—a strange sound to hear, like the rasping of two branches together.

Nokomis clapped her hands and the others nodded and even Quill yelled "Howah!" at the sound of Omakayas's new name.

SIX

THE PATH OF BUTTERFLIES

They woke covered by a blanket of yellow butterflies. Thousands of wings had fluttered down on them by night, and as the sun rose and warmed the creatures, they skipped everywhere—across the sand, over the light waves. Hundreds fanned their wings on the damp bark of the canoes, on the packs. They clung to the cooking pots, flitted around the baskets, and the blankets were covered with bright golden wings. The butterflies had black smudges on their wings that looked like staring eyes, and their wings were edged in soft black, too. With every movement the family made, the butterflies swirled up in a dance of light. Omakayas almost hated to leave them.

Bizheens put his hands up in wonder and waved his fingers. The butterflies landed on his hair, his arms, his little hands, even the tip of his tiny nose. Bizheens tried to catch and eat the butterflies at first, but at last he gave up and batted at their wings in play. The butterflies poured off Deydey's shoulders as he worked to load the canoes.

"This is a good sign from the Great Kind Spirit who loves us all," said Nokomis. "This is like a smile from the Creator, my children."

And the truth was everyone was smiling, even Quill, even Old Tallow. Who could help smiling when visited by these beautiful and fragile spirits? Only the dogs belonging to Old Tallow took little notice.

As the family pushed out onto the water, to cross the lake, a brilliant cloud of yellow wings followed them a short way, then disappeared, like a soft good-bye.

As they crossed the lake, paddling, their spirits lifted. The way was long, but they would find their family in the end. The family sang together, back and forth between the canoes. They sang traveling songs, surprise songs, nonsense songs, even a love song from Deydey to Mama, who laughed and flicked water backward at him from her paddle. Bizheens loved the surprise of the canoe and put his hands on the gunwales and his face into the wind. He laughed with happiness, and Omakayas laughed with him and kissed him. Once, looking up at Miskobines, she saw the old man smiling to see how much she loved her little brother. Paddling behind his father, Animikiins was smiling at her too, and she looked quickly down and hid her face in her baby brother's hair. Bizheens pulled at her braids, and she made a quiet game of counting his fingers to keep him from throwing the canoe off balance. That was her job—amusing lively Bizheens.

The lake was big, shallow, and sandy for a long way out, then deep and calm. The sun was much higher by the time they could see the other shore, but as land came into view they could all see that something was happening in the sky.

Their paddles dipped more slowly, then stopped, for the sky ahead was turning a gray color that had nothing to do with clouds or the weather. Deydey said it looked like fire, and Old Tallow nodded. In the heat of midsummer, lightning struck trees that burst into flames, or sometimes mounds of deep rotting wood kindled all by themselves. White settlers, would-be farmers, also started fires to clear fields or pastures. But the woods were so dry by the middle of the summer that even campfires weren't safe. Everything was dry tinder, ready to catch fire. The whole family had been extremely careful in putting out their fires as they moved through the woods.

They approached this lake's far shore carefully, but at last they were in shallow water. As they drew their canoes close to the opposite shore, where they would prepare to portage all their belongings to the next lake over, Old Tallow suddenly signaled them to hush.

Her dogs were standing motionless in her canoe, hackles raised, staring at the screen of brush and trees just past the shoreline. The leaves were thick, and there was no doubt in Old Tallow's mind that something—more likely, someone—was concealed there. Whoever it was would have seen them approach for miles. Someone was waiting to ambush them. Once all of their canoes were ashore, they would be helpless on the wide expanse of sand.

Instantly, everyone except Old Tallow pushed back off-shore and hunkered down in their canoes. Omakayas curled around Bizheens, who seemed to understand something was wrong and went tense and silent, watchful too. Mama both steered and paddled as Deydey pulled out his gun. Miskobines, Animikiins, Fishtail, and even Quill took out their bows and fitted arrows instantly into their hands. Old Tallow motioned to them that she was going to go ashore first. She had her gun loaded and her spear at her side. She got out of her canoe and crept onto the sandy shore, her dogs in a circle around her. Suddenly the gray female, always the boldest, bounded forward and disappeared into the brush. Old Tallow crouched down, ready for an attack, but instead of an impressive Bwaan warrior, a young chimookoman stumbled out onto the sand with the gray dog holding tight to the leg of his breeches.

"Call him off! Please!" the boy cried. "We're lost! Help us!"

Old Tallow, who did not understand the English language, kept her gun trained on the boy. Deydey knew what he was saying and told Mama to bring the canoe close enough to shore for him to land. Deydey got out of the canoe holding his gun and waded over to stand next to Old Tallow.

"Tell all of your people to come out of hiding," said Deydey, in English, to the skinny little boy, who wore dirty, tattered clothing and was no more than six or seven winters old. "We will not harm you."

The boy's blackened face trembled as he tried to hold back his emotions. "There is only my little sister," he said. He turned and whistled sweetly as a bird and called, "Susan!" A tiny little girl toddled out of the leaves. She wore a halo of soft red hair just like her brother, but she was so young that she had just begun to walk. Her face

was also dark with dirt, and she gazed at everyone soberly as she sucked on her hand.

"Your mother, your father, your family?" asked Deydey.

The boy turned away, hiding his face. He told Deydey that he and his little sister had come to the lake where at least they could find water. For a long time, said the boy, they'd had nothing to eat but a young robin, which the boy was proud to have caught, and a few turtle eggs they had dug out of the sand.

"Howah," said Old Tallow, patting the boy's shoulder when Deydey told her about the turtle eggs and the robin. "You are a mighty hunter. You provided for your little sister."

Deydey asked the little boy where their parents were. He offered to find them. But the boy shook his head and slumped down suddenly on his knees. The memory was too much for him. He said that he and his little sister had been sleeping on the floor of their cabin, and awakened one morning to find it full of smoke.

"We tried to wake our mother and father," he said, "but they would not move."

The parents had been sleeping higher up, on a platform. The smoke had risen and collected all around them, but the floor was clear. The two children had stayed by their mother and father, trying to wake them, until the fire became so hot, and the smoke so thick, that they'd had to flee.

Old Tallow knelt down near the boy and continued to pat his sharp trembling shoulders. The little girl stared at them all with round blue eyes as her brother went on talking. It didn't look like they'd been on their own for more than a couple of days. They were skinny, but their bones weren't showing yet. They were covered with bug bites and sores. From the looks of the sky, the fire was still burning and had come closer. They could now smell the sharp smoke on the wind.

Nokomis waded to shore with a bag of the pounded venison and berries that Omakayas had made. She opened the bag and gestured to the boy and the little girl, then pretended to eat.

"It is good," said Deydey. "Pemmican. Eat it!"

The boy reached in first and took a handful. He ate the

good pemmican as slowly as he could, but he was clearly famished, and soon he and his little sister began to wolf the food down, handful after handful, eyeing Nokomis to assess the moment she would close the mouth of the sack. But slowly and gently, she lowered the sack to the ground and made its opening wider. Old Tallow was already busy making a little cooking fire, and she had sent Animikiins and his father, along with Quill, away with the dogs to investigate the woods and make sure they were safe.

"Bring back a waabooz, or a fat squirrel," she had ordered. "Let's feed them up and then go looking for their family."

NIGHT ON FIRE

They wouldn't have a chance to find the children's family for days, however, because suddenly the wind changed direction. Smoke billowed up over the trees. A black veil covered the sun, and the air grew thick with falling ash. Everyone scrambled back into the three canoes—the lost children both got in with Nokomis, Fishtail, and Angeline. Old Tallow and her dogs took Animikiins and Miskobines in their canoe. Deydey, Mama, Quill, Omakayas, and Bizheens piled into their canoe and the whole family paddled out onto the lake, just past the reach of smoke. From there, as the sun set, casting a stark radiance through the smoke and the flames, they watched the woods burn steadily toward them.

It seemed like the whole night was on fire. Hot winds from shore sickened everyone, and the smoke hung down in a choking mass. The grown-ups took turns lying down in the bottoms of the canoes, but they were cramped and could not stretch out. Quill, whose porcupine coughed on top of his head, slept sitting up with his arms folded for a while, then slowly wedged himself into the front of the canoe. It was better for Omakayas and Bizheens, who lay in the bottom and breathed cooler air. Deydey and Old Tallow roped each canoe to the next one and made a small flotilla. The waves were calm enough so that there was no danger of capsizing, and with one or two of the grown-ups keeping watch they drifted around in the middle of the lake.

Halfway through the night, with everyone awake, the family gave up sleeping and began to talk. The presence of the pitiful settlers' children had reminded Deydey of something he rarely mentioned. His father had been a trader, his mother of the Anishinabe people. He gazed at the children in Fishtail's canoe and at one point shook his head and said, "I feel very sad for these lost ones. I was lucky my mother's people adopted me, and my uncle became my father and loved me as a father does. My own father, who was mostly white like these children, did not love me."

"Did you ever know your father?" asked Quill.

This was a question that nobody else would have dared ask, for the very mention of Deydey's father had in the past caused his brows to lower, his eyes to flash. But this was a special night. A night they had to endure together, and so Deydey answered this question for the very first time.

"Geget," said Deydey, "I met my father once. And I never cared to meet him again."

Quill was quiet and his porcupine slept peacefully. Everyone else would have left off with the subject, but not Quill.

"Deydey," he said, "will you tell me about meeting your father?"

Now Deydey's eyes did flash and harden. The fire glinted across his face.

"I will tell you," he said in a soft and somehow dangerous voice. "And then you will know why I loved my mother and my uncle, why my grandmother speaks to me in my dreams, and why I do not trust the white people.

Here is how it happened."

Then Deydey told how all of his life his mother had prepared him to meet his father by teaching him what little French she knew. She told him that his father was a rich and important man, and that he had loved her. She told him that his father would love his son, because he had loved her so greatly. His father had gone away into his country but would return, she said. When this great man did return, she taught his son to be ready. Deydey's mother taught him how to behave like a white person. How to bow, how to shake hands, how to look at people's eyes, how to show his teeth in a bold, strange smile. She and her father taught him how to play chess, which he liked very much. She also taught him the words to say when he met his father, *Vous êtes mon père.* You are my father. He repeated the words, learned them, and looked forward to the proud day when he would walk up to his father and announce himself. He pictured his father bending down then, and taking him into his arms.

"But it did not happen that way," Deydey said.

The day did come. When Deydey was ten years old, his mother learned that the rich trader who had loved her was journeying toward a fort one hundred miles north. Deydey and his mother walked those hundred miles. When they reached the fort, they were allowed to enter. The great man was in the central compound, smoking after a meal with his friends. Deydey's mother begged that her son be allowed to enter the house, and one of the voyageurs took Deydey to the entrance. He knocked on the door and was invited to enter.

When he was standing in the room, five men by the fire turned to look at him. They were all surprised to see the boy, who looked them all over proudly, one by one. Suddenly, said Deydey, he knew who his father was. He walked straight up to the most powerful man in the room. The man was the one the others deferred to, the one seated in the middle. Deydey said that he held out his hand to shake that man's hand, then he smiled. His heart was open. Deydey said that he did exactly what his mother had taught him to do.

"Vous êtes mon père," he said.

The well-dressed man reared back, looked at the other men, then opened his mouth and began to laugh. The other men looked astounded but also sly, and they soon began to laugh too. Their laughter soared, grew hysterical. They slapped their thighs, wept at the absurdity. Their laughter carried them away.

"I walked out of that place," said Deydey, "and back to my mother. And that was the only time I saw my father."

Everyone was silent after Deydey finished speaking, and then Quill said, in a way that impressed Omakayas as very grown-up, kind, and unlike the Quill she knew: "Deydey, I am glad you left that man and went with your mother. For I am proud to be your son and an Anishinabe."

* * *

They waited out in the canoes until rain put the fires out the next day. Only then did they dare paddle onto shore again. This time, the land looked sadly different. The trees stood out black in the drizzle, most of them great leafless sticks. Some had toppled or crumbled to ash. Animals lay dead on shore—a deer, a fox, their fur singed and burned away. As they drew their canoes up, the family noticed how hot the sand just underneath the wet surface was—it still contained the last ferocity of the fire.

They camped there all the same, and the next morning, Deydey and Fishtail decided to try searching out the homestead in the direction that the boy thought he had come from. They were gone all day. When they came back, Deydey said under his breath that they had not found a single trace of the cabin. He also said that everything, everywhere, for miles and miles, as far as they could see, was thoroughly burnt. There was nothing left. And no one.

So it happened that the family was unexpectedly enlarged by two. Angeline prepared a more comfortable place in their canoe for the chimookoman children and there they crouched, miserable but safe. Perhaps a trader would know of their parents, perhaps a priest farther north would take them in. But before they could find someone who might know the children, the family would have to carry their canoes overland. They would have to portage through the devastation.

Old Tallow fitted up her red dog with a carrier for the girl. She kept her gray and black dogs alongside her for hunting. She cut two poles for the drags and tied a deerskin between them. She used strips of hide to harness this contraption to the dog, then tied the little girl onto the deer hide. She relied on her dogs to alert her to any other strangers they might meet along the way. Once they got past the fire, that is. This was still the season of raids and war parties, and Old Tallow was determined that nobody should catch her family unaware.

SEVEN

TRAIL OF ASH

This was the opposite of the way lit by butterflies, Omakayas decided as she lugged Bizheens, a bag of pemmican, a small ax, a pack of dried meat, and a bale of beaver skins along the portage to the next lake. Heavy loads were just part of life when you traveled by water. There would always come a shore, and a portage between lake or river to the next shore. Nobody thought twice about it, but Omakayas now fantasized that they would find a swift river that would transport them all the way to Lac du Bois. How marvelous—a calm rapids like a smooth road for the canoes. She saw it in her mind, curving through the heavy forests and sunny clearings. They'd be there in days, maybe hours! She couldn't wait to see her cousin Twilight's calm and shining face. As for Amoosens, would Little Bee have grown tall, or stout like her mother, Muskrat?

After her dream about Two Strike's wonderful fish, she realized that seeing Two Strike would be complicated. But you had to take the good along with the not-so-good, she thought. With her strong, new name held close inside, perhaps she would be so grown-up and adult now that Two Strike's ways would seem merely childish irritations.

The way was difficult, although the undergrowth was burned away. Everyone's legs and hands soon turned black with the tremendous soot. Ash muffled each footstep, and clouds of ash puffed out around each step. The ash sifted down their backs, crept up their legs and sleeves, and itched terribly. It was impossible to scratch those itches while carrying a heavy load. The woods around them were smoldering charcoal. They choked and spat as they walked. Luckily, it was not a long way to the next lake, and there was a river passage out of that one. By the time they did get to the water, they were covered with ash, like ghostly beings, and their chests hurt. They coughed for days after passing through the aftermath of that fire.

But the way turned green again, and soon they were traveling up a river lushly overgrown with trees right to the banks. The trees hung over the water in a pretty canopy, but the undergrowth made everyone uneasy. Soon enough, when the river ended in a tiny lake, and they crossed the lake, they were on a well-worn path. On this path, said Deydey in a worried voice, they would be sure to meet others.

WARRIORS

When they had traveled for about a mile, Old Tallow, who walked ahead with her dogs, motioned for everyone to halt, then to hide. It wasn't easy lugging the canoes off the trail and trying to disappear with all of their packs and belongings, but the dogs clearly sensed someone coming far ahead, and it was wise to decide from a hidden place whether that someone was friendly.

Not friendly!

Everyone hunkered close to earth. Here were the people they had dreaded meeting all along. A party of Bwaanag, handsome and powerful men, painted for revenge, stalked quietly along the path. There were so many recent footprints on that part of the trail that theirs would not stand out. They could stay unnoticed, unless someone made a sound. Hidden in the underbrush, everyone breathed quietly. Old Tallow had her hands on her dogs' snouts and they knew better than to yip or yowl. Even Bizheens knew better than to make a sound when everyone was tense and quiet. Quill's porcupine, of course, was sleeping happily upon Quill's head. The only one who might give their position away was the little girl the dog had drawn along. The little sprite beamed with smiles and her red hair flamed among the trees. Quickly, Omakayas saw her older sister cover the girl's head with a blanket and slip a lump of maple sugar from her pack. Smiling at the child, Angeline popped a few grains into her mouth. The girl's eyes went round with happy surprise and she sucked in peace, with no idea in the world how close to danger she and the family were.

Had it always been this way? Omakayas wondered as the Bwaanag passed. They were a striking people, every one of them—tall, slender, strong as buffalo bows, and graceful as birds of prey. Strange and beautiful designs, sharp-edged and complicated, were quilled and beaded into their clothing. One wore yellow paint and another wore vermilion in bold designs. They were focused, dangerous. Omakayas closed her eyes and pictured a hawk plunging from the sky. Had the Bwaanag always been frightening enemies? She knew that her own people sent war parties into Bwaan country and came back with deaths to boast of, with horses, or with captives to replace any Anishinabeg victims who had been lost to a war party the previous summer. Yet there were some, also, who traded with the Bwaanag and knew their language—and others, like her Deydey, who believed that the real enemy they all faced was the growing threat of white settlers. The chimookomanag didn't care whose hunting land they stepped on, Bwaanag or Anishinabeg— they stole it all the same.

The family stayed in the woods for a long time after the Bwaanag passed, but eventually the dogs relaxed their guard and it seemed safe to return to their path. They traveled for the rest of the day, still hoping to find water again, cross it, and make their way to a place far from the trail to camp in safety. But the hiding had delayed them and so they were forced to stop. They settled far from the trail and ate cold pemmican, for fear a sturdy blaze would bring the war party back their way. They were spooked and watchful.

Still, it was dusk, a good time for boys to hunt. Fishtail and Deydey had dammed up a little stream and were catching trout. While they were busy, Quill and Animikiins decided to travel back down the path not only to see if they could bring down an animal, but also to make sure that the Bwaanag were not creeping up behind them. They told Old Tallow they were going, and she frowned.

"Gego ginjiba'iweken," she said. "Ask Nokomis or ask your mother. You must stay."

But, because she was busy with repairs to a canoe, they managed to creep around her and elude her strict attention.

Omakayas was to remember, for a very long time, how

their leaving together bothered her. For some reason, as the two boys walked away, their jokes and quiet smiles chilled her. She *knew*, absolutely *knew* in her heart, that something was going to go wrong. She ran after them. They turned to her.

"Don't go," she said.

They just smiled and kept walking. It was useless. Without knowing she would do it, she gave the flint and striker in her special pouch to Quill, even though she'd carried them every day since she was capable of making fire. Her precious string of red beads, she gave to Animikiins. This was the second time she had given these beads away, and she wondered at her impulses. Nokomis had kept them for many, many years.

"What," mocked Quill, his porcupine wagging on his head, "is this good-bye forever?"

"Don't go," she begged again.

Animikiins took the beads from her hands with a shy smile—this could almost be a love gift. They both knew it meant she favored him, but they were friends already. Omakayas shrugged, trying not to make too much of it, but she said "Don't go" for the last time, in a smaller voice.

"You know we'll go anyway," said Quill, just loud enough for her to hear. His porcupine blinked. "I have a better idea. Keep your beads and don't worry!"

Animikiins just smiled at her and put the beads around his neck. Then the two strong boys loped off into the woods along the trail. Omakayas couldn't help but smile at the way the porcupine's tail wagged along behind Quill's head. How could anything bad happen to someone so ridiculous?

MISSING

They did not return. When the night came on, Mama worried, but the boys had stayed out all night before when trailing a wounded animal.

"Maybe they are tracking a deer," she said hopefully.

Deydey and Old Tallow took the dogs out to follow them, and Fishtail made his own search, but the way soon grew too dark and dangerous. They all returned with no sight of the two boys. Yet there had also been no sign of the Bwaan warriors, and everybody hoped the boys had simply decided to stay the night where they'd made a kill. The family curled in their blankets and tried to drift off, but it was a sleepless night. One of the adults kept watch every hour, and from time to time, restless, Omakayas woke in the dark to see her mother outlined against the pale sky. The moon had risen, wild and full, and the boys had enough light to see by if they needed to return.

But they were still gone in the morning. Now everyone was grim. Nokomis prayed, her hand on a birch tree, her lips moving softly. Old Tallow prepared herself and fed her dogs. Fishtail and Deydey cleaned their guns and Miskobines examined his bow and readied a quiver of arrows. They all carried axes and stone or steel tomahawks at their belts. They were going after the boys and did not know what they'd find. But they were leaving the little ones in the care of the women. Yellow Kettle knew that she and the other women might put up a good fight, but they'd be overwhelmed by the party of Bwaanag if they doubled back and attacked them. To throw the Bwaanag off their trail, she proposed that the men leave the canoes in the woods beside a smoking fire, and the women would find another hiding place farther back, brushing out their tracks as they went.

The little boy, John, whose name always came out Zahn, worked as hard as anyone readying the supplies. He was a good-natured boy still in shock, in grief, and Angeline's heart was very soft for him. She kept him with her, and took care of the baby, Susan, whose name in the Anishinabe tongue came out Zozed. Zahn and Zozed. They were both good children and Omakayas felt sorry for them, losing their parents. She did not want to lose anyone, and she was very scared of what might happen to the men and Old Tallow on the trail.

She had no idea they'd be gone for so very long.

EIGHT

THE CAPTURE

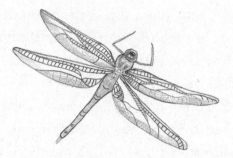

The moon was full when the boys left, and full a month
later when Old Tallow returned with her dogs. Many
things happened in that time. The women made a new
camp. They replenished their store of dried meat. They
fished and trapped. They found a rice bay and busied
themselves harvesting every grain. Dragonflies had lifted
and hovered over the rice. They seemed friendly, comforting. Omakayas had whispered to them messages of love
for the men and for Old Tallow. In all that time, they saw
no sign of the Bwaanag. The women did what they could
to work hard, and tried their best not to despair. But on
the afternoon when they saw Old Tallow walk into camp

alone, Yellow Kettle, Nokomis, Omakayas, and Angeline fell to the ground in fear. Before anyone could ask, Old Tallow cried out, "Captured!

"But all is not lost, thanks to your Deydey," she quickly said. "The men are two days behind me. They have Quill."

Mama howled with joy and threw herself on Old Tallow, who patted her awkwardly. Nokomis sat on the ground, breathing hard, weeping along with Omakayas, who was terrified to ask what had happened to Animikiins and his father.

"They would not release Animikiins," Old Tallow said softly.

Everyone was silent.

"Fishtail?" asked Angeline weakly.

"He returns," said Old Tallow. "Here is how it went." She settled herself and her dogs. Nokomis gave her a makak of water and some pemmican. "We trailed them all the way to their camp out in the flat world, the Plains," continued Old Tallow. "Your Deydey walked up to the enemy camp alone. Howah! His courage astounded the Bwaanag, and the council chief who had called the war party came forward."

Nokomis, Mama, Angeline, and Omakayas sat down to listen to Old Tallow. Zahn took his little sister and Bizheens away—he was very good at amusing them, and he was even beginning to learn some of the Anishinabe language.

OLD TALLOW'S STORY

The chief and Deydey agreed to have peaceful talks, and then the rest of us appeared. I don't think they could tell that I was a woman, because when I sat down they didn't flinch away. They were interested to see me.

The chief and Deydey smoked the pipe. It was found that the Bwaanag were not out for war. They were searching for a captive to replace the chief's son. He had been lost one year ago, to our people.

"When we first saw this boy with the porcupine on his head," said the chief, "we were mystified. We watched him for a long time, and then decided that his medicine must be very great. He was hard to capture. His porcupine fought with him. Our warriors were covered with his arrows."

"Yes," said Deydey to the Bwaan. Deydey was the only one of us who spoke their language, so he translated what the Bwaan chief said. His eyes lighted with pride at his son's strength. As for me, I was caught between pride and laughter, even in that dangerous situation. I could not help but think of Quill's great battle—his porcupine swiping at the Bwaanag warriors from the top of his master's head. Deydey continued to speak.

"I can see that you are brokenhearted, and that my people are responsible. But if you take my son or the son of Miskobines, then we will be brokenhearted."

"Why should that matter to us?" asked the chief, with scorn.

"Because it will cause us to raise a war party and someone in your village will surely die."

"Yes, that is true, but we are not afraid."

"See into my fatherly heart," said Deydey, "and know that I have never hurt one of your people. I have never made war against your people. I have traded with and admired you. I do not want to kill you and I do not want you to kill my sons, or me, or my party here. I think we can find another way."

"What way is that?" said the chief.

The two smoked their pipes and were lost in contemplation for quite some time. Nobody thought they would come to a solution. Then Deydey said, "We will adopt each other. We will become brothers. We will enter your clan, and you will enter ours. We will bring gifts to you, and honor you. For one year, you will have me, my son, and his medicine animal to console you. The next year, my son and I will return to our family."

I could tell how deeply it hurt him to make this offer. I could see that tears shone in his eyes. But he spoke clearly, and said, "We could do more, at peace."

The war chief was impressed with this offer, and called his council. While they talked, however, Miskobines came forward and raised his arm, and then he spoke, and Deydey translated.

"Hear me, hear me, all of you! My son is named for the thunders, and he is a fine son. I love him more than I love my own life. My son, Animikiins, has offered to be the son of the chief instead of Quill. He says that Quill is not yet old enough, nor is the porcupine upon his head."

The chief smiled in spite of himself.

"Animikiins, named for the thunders, has said that he will take his place. For my part, as his father, I offer to adopt you also. I offer to live for one year as the hunter in a family who has lost a man. I am still strong, I can still draw a bow, and I have the wisdom of these gray hairs. I am not done with my existence yet! I will live here for a year only to help the Bwaanag. Then my son and I will return to our people."

"Why," said the chief, "if I take a liking to this boy, and he looks like a fine, strong boy, should I agree to let him go?"

Then Animikiins turned bold. He spoke.

"Because," he said, holding up the red beads that *someone* had given him, "I promised to return these to a girl!"

When this was translated to the Bwaanag, they burst out laughing and slapped Animikiins on the back and made jokes. And then we had a great feast and they gave the men new sets of clothing—they figured me out and gave me a dress, which I saved for Nokomis here—and after quite a few more days of getting to know one another we took our leave of those people. They were surprisingly good people. Sisseton and Wahpeton, they call themselves. Very generous, though still fearsome.

Old Tallow reached into her pack and shook out a beautiful dress made of white doeskin. The skin was fluffy and light as cloth, beaded blue and orange across the yoke. It had deep fringe and was created with admirably tiny stitches.

"Hmmph," said Nokomis, "their women can sew." She accepted the dress and held it in her arms. "But they can't have our boy, and they can't have the old man, either!"

Still, it was a great relief to know that the men were alive, and everyone slept more soundly than they had for an entire moon.

* * *

When Deydey, Fishtail, and Quill arrived, everyone gathered around, hugging them, amazed and tearful. Angeline was almost faint with relief, and all of her love showed in her face, increasing her beauty to such a degree that she seemed to blaze in the fresh light. From her pack, she drew Fishtail's wedding vest. At once, he put it on and then the two stared into each other's eyes. Feeling much older, but still in love, they stood holding each other in gratitude.

Yellow Kettle always confused her affection with anger, and even as she put her head against Deydey's chest, she gave a furious shake of her hand at Quill and cuffed at him before he darted away. The porcupine tumbled off his head, and Nokomis took the opportunity to grab Quill in a hug, so there was nothing he could do but hug her back. Omakayas stood aside and tried not to feel anything but the happiness of seeing her father and brother, but part of her was bereft. She missed Animikiins and Miskobines. She wondered if she'd ever see the boy who seemed to understand her, or the old man with his great sense of thoughtful dignity.

"They will return," said Deydey, as if he knew what she was thinking. "The Bwaan chief promised that they would be back by next spring."

Omakayas turned her head shyly, in confusion that her feelings were noticed, and when she did she stared

directly into the eyes of the chimookoman boy. Zahn stood motionless with his little sister, watching the reunion. There was no doubt that he, too, was happy to see Deydey and Quill. But in his face there was also an intense longing—for his own parents, surely. Omakayas instantly felt a pang of grief for him. She walked over, put her arms around his shoulders, and said that he was a brave boy. He didn't yet understand enough of the Ojibwe language to reply, but he seemed to know that she cared for him. His hand tightened on her wrist.

NINE

PUSHING ON

Deydey and Quill lifted the canoe that belonged to Miskobines and Animikiins up into a tree, where it wouldn't rot, and where Miskobines and his son would find it when they returned from the Bwaanag. As the family traveled, they suffered from the loss of two hunters. Old Miskobines had the wily patience of age, and Animikiins had great strength and endurance. The family moved north. The area they passed through was well hunted, and as the birds and geese were now moving south it was increasingly hard to find meat. But it was a good rice year, and great stands of manoomin fed them along the way. They reached the south shore of

Miskwaagamiiwi, or Red Lake, and with great relief traveled along its edge, making a good distance every day, and stuffing themselves with fish. The days were long and perfectly warm, but at night there was a chill. In the morning, there was a fresh vigor to the air.

Soon, too soon, the leaves would fall. Already, Omakayas could see the first signs of dagwaaging, autumn, in the initial flags of red, orange, and yellow in the maples and birch.

Old Tallow had her dogs, Nokomis, and the white children in her small canoe. Deydey and Mama traveled with Omakayas and Bizheens. Fishtail, Angeline, and Quill paddled a new canoe, which they had just made as best they could. They were all wedged in surrounded by packs of furs and bark packs of manoomin, bags of weyass, dried meat, or pemmican, pots, tanned skins, and bundles of their blankets. All summer, they had added to their store of goods, which they planned to trade for new traps, heavy blankets, ammunition. They had never been loaded with such wealth, and were very careful not to wet the packs of furs and hides. There would be so much to carry once they reached the northern tip of Red Lake that they worried about how they would make it across the great stretch of waabashkiki, or swampland, that still lay between the little family and the great lake where Muskrat lived.

"We have come at the right time," said Deydey, "before the rains begin. But we must hurry, or we will have to wait until freeze-up to cross the sloughs and bogs."

Every day they paddled the loaded canoes for as long as they could. When they camped onshore at night, they sometimes put up lean-tos of leafy branches. Other nights, they dug comfortable beds in the sand and slept curled in their blankets. Most of the mosquitoes and flies were gone now, and the peaceful waves curled all night at their feet.

The little porcupine had grown into a fat waddling creature and often wandered away at night. But every morning, when Quill awakened, his medicine animal would be crouched beside his blanket, snoring softly. When he rose, the porcupine would follow him to the fire and sit beside him. Quill would share his first food of the day—some wild rice, a bit of stew, whatever he had. The porcupine especially liked tea now that the weather was getting cool. Nokomis prepared rich swamp tea from a shiny leaf with a dull brown underside and added a little maple sugar to the tin cup everybody shared. The porcupine always got the sweet dregs. It would sit, balanced on its threatening tail, and hold the cup in its plump dark paws. Quill had taught it to drink the tea, and after it drank the sweetness it always gave a tiny sigh of happiness. Then it would throw the cup down and waddle away.

Mama said that it wouldn't be long before the porcupine

did not return, and that made Omakayas feel sad about the passing of things. Not only that, but since Quill had returned from the Bwaanag, he had become surprisingly quiet and serious, and he avoided Omakayas the way boys, as they grew older, avoided their sisters. She was surprised that she missed his teasing ways, but she did, and often looked over at him paddling with Fishtail and wished that he would make a face at her or splash her or even laugh at her. So she felt an unexpected happiness when he woke her one morning with an insult.

"What's this old root that drifted up last night?" he said, kicking at her foot.

She kicked back at him, sleepily, and sat up rubbing the sleep off her face.

"It's your sister," she said, "the one you have forgotten."

"It is you," said Quill slowly, "who will soon forget me."

They looked at each other for a moment, upset at their own feelings, then Quill bugged his eyes out, stretched his lips with his fingers, made a horrible cackling noise, and began to pelt her with leaves and sticks. Omakayas felt better immediately and jumped up to start the day, which, as it happened, would be one that she'd long remember.

THE RAID

It began with a hearty boozhoo from the woods as they were settling their packs and kettles into their canoes. Omakayas was helping Old Tallow pack her canoe, and she had just settled Zahn and Zozed in among the goods that they would carry. All of the canoes were pulled just barely ashore, ready at any moment to shove off, when the boozhoo sounded again.

"I know that voice," said Old Tallow. "And I don't like it."

Soon the leaves parted and none other than Albert LaPautre appeared, the husband of Auntie Muskrat and father of Omakayas's cousins. He was round as a barrel, with tiny eyes sharp with greed, and wore his hair in two long braids. LaPautre was vain about his clothing and always had to have the nattiest vests and fanciest silver pins and armbands. However, this day, although he looked to have dressed himself in what he considered finery, there was something wretched about his appearance. Strings of tattered ribbon hung from his shirt, and his pants were held up with a sash that shone with grease. The family hadn't seen him since they had all left the island together. After only a few days, Albert LaPautre had persuaded Auntie Muskrat to take a different route north.

Although Old Tallow held herself still and her dogs growled suspiciously, Omakayas was happy to see her uncle because it meant, she hoped, that her cousins would be near. But Albert LaPautre appeared to be alone. She dropped the bundle she was carrying and went forward to greet her uncle.

Deydey also approached Albert and asked about the rest of the family.

"I am surprised to see you here," added Mama, who was holding Bizheens by the hand. She had just put most of her cooking equipment into the canoe she would paddle with Deydey. "Where is my sister?" she asked.

"Where is my daughter?" echoed Nokomis.

"Where are my cousins?" said Quill and Omakayas together.

Fishtail and Angeline, who had just finished packing their canoe, left it barely touching the sand and walked over to Albert, also curious.

Albert disregarded their questions. His eyes darted with great interest to the family's packs of furs and hides and manoomin, but then he narrowed his eyes, pretending indifference. He looked away and put a pleasant, eager expression on his face. Omakayas could see that there was something wrong. He seemed jittery, his voice was pinched.

"You have been hard at work, I see. Are you on your way to the trader's?" He gave a hollow, jolly laugh.

Old Tallow and her dogs stepped closer, next to Deydey.

"Are your ears shut? Let me ask you again," she said in a menacing voice. "Where is your family?"

"Oh, ah, they are all very well, doing very well, ah yes, up in Lac du Bois, up there in the islands. Good hunting, fishing. Yes, they are fine."

Sweat popped out on Albert LaPautre's big shiny face and his eyes darted from side to side, shifty and strange. One of Old Tallow's dogs growled at the bushes behind Albert, and Old Tallow raised her hatchet.

"Who is with you?" said Deydey.

"Eh, nobody." Albert opened his mouth in an oily grin and stepped closer. Omakayas noticed that he'd lost several teeth. All of a sudden, he lunged, caught Old Tallow around the middle, and knocked her to the ground. At once, the dogs were on top of him, growling and tearing at his arms and legs. Another dog darted into the bushes, a cry of pain was heard, and then a gun fired. Deydey was wearing his cloth turban, and it flew off as he fell backward.

Omakayas threw herself on the ground and crawled to her father. Fishtail and Quill ran forward to meet two other men, scrawny and desperate, who leaped from the undergrowth. Nokomis unsheathed her knife and ran at one man, but Yellow Kettle got to him first. She grabbed a rice knocker and began to lambast him while Angeline used a paddle to beat him from behind. When yet another man reached from the bush and grabbed Omakayas's foot, she slashed his hand with her knife and scrambled to her father's side.

LaPautre saw his chance and tried to escape. Running at him with a fierce war yell, Quill tripped on a root. As he fell, his pet porcupine lost its grip on his head and went flying, a prickly cannonball, straight into LaPautre's face. Now LaPautre's cry went up, a bizarre and shocked howl. Plucking madly at his cheeks and neck, he ran smack into a tree. He staggered away, lolling crazily from side to side, then gained his balance and dived into the brush. By the time Quill had picked himself up, all of the attackers were gone.

"Howah," Quill said to his porcupine, gently rubbing its nose, "you are a brave warrior."

Omakayas cradled her father's head. His face was torn and bleeding, but he was talking and gesturing with his

hands. Nokomis and Yellow Kettle bent over him and traced how the bullet from the gun had creased his scalp. There were black powder burns all around his eyes and he couldn't open them.

"Help, help!" It was Zahn, yelling from the canoe as he tried to fight off the men, who had sneaked around along the shore. Omakayas turned to see them—four ragged Anishinabeg and mixed-bloods and one white man. They had leaped into the canoes and were trying to shove off. LaPautre, still popping with quills, was desperately trying to join his fellow thieves.

There was a fierce yell from Fishtail.

"Get them!"

Old Tallow ran to the shore along with Omakayas and Quill. The attackers had taken advantage of the family's fear over Deydey and managed to shove off with everything, including Zahn and Zozed, with their furs, their skins, their blankets, their kettles, except for the one Mama had grabbed to swing at the head of one of the attackers. Nokomis yelled, "Go!" Fishtail, Angeline, Yellow Kettle, Quill, and Omakayas flung themselves into the lake and swam as hard as they could. Zahn struggled with the attackers and Omakayas saw one of them strike the boy, who fell into the bottom of the canoe. They swam with mad energy, but the wind was with the paddlers and they slowly outdistanced even Angeline, the fastest swimmer.

At last, they were left treading water. Everything was gone. The canoes were quickly vanishing and only Zozed's thin wail could be heard. The sound of that little cry struck them all to their hearts. Omakayas shouted over and over to Zahn, but there was no answer. The canoes were only black dots. Turning to one another, swimming back in shock, the family saw that in one instant they had gone from having everything they needed, to having nothing.

And worse than that, Deydey was blinded by the flash of powder from the gun.

TEN

WHAT WAS LEFT

"Hold still," said Nokomis impatiently. She was bathing Deydey's face and eyes with warm tea brewed from the needles and roots of balsam trees. They had made camp on the north shore of the big lake. Now there was no question that they would have to wait until freeze-up to cross the great waabashkiki, the swamp that stretched before them. It was terrible to see Deydey stumbling about, his eyes wrapped, or hanging on to the arm of Yellow Kettle. He still could not see, but Nokomis made him lie still as often as she could, bathed his eyes, and counseled him to have patience.

During the robbery, Fishtail had grabbed his gun, but

had little ammunition. The women still had their knives. Omakayas had been rolling up her blanket, so she had something to keep her warm, which she now shared with Bizheens. Mama had her one kettle and a rice knocker. Old Tallow had her dogs. At that moment, Old Tallow and her dogs were out hunting with a spear she'd made by tying her knife to a heavy stick. She was determined to bring down a bear for its meat and fur. Old Tallow missed the coat that became her blanket, her shelter once the wind grew cold. That coat had been made of furs and velvets, calico patches, and patterned wool blankets. It had been Old Tallow's favorite possession and she vowed that if she ever found Albert LaPautre she would skin him alive and add his pelt to her collection.

Omakayas knew she actually meant that. She shuddered but felt in her own heart there was no revenge harsh enough for what LaPautre had done.

"What will they do with Zahn, with Zozed?" she asked every day.

Everyone had a different idea. Deydey was sure that LaPautre would try to ransom them off to a trader and say that he had rescued them. Fishtail had whispered his fear that they would be sold, as servants, to some farm family. Nokomis believed that they would be rescued somehow. Everyone had a conflicting opinion, but their hearts were wrenched. Angeline, especially, had grown fond of the children. She and Fishtail had planned to adopt them in a ceremony once they reached a new home place.

"At least," said Angeline, "if they were sold to a trader or a priest, they would not starve." Right now, that was a distinct possibility for them all. They had faced starvation before, but never without their guns and traps. Omakayas could not imagine what would happen to them if Deydey's eyes did not heal. His cheeks were still blackened, his forehead still bruised green and dark yellow. The worst thing was, the question "Why?" had no answer. LaPautre had been ridiculous, pompous, and an embarrassment sometimes. He'd neglected his family and believed himself a famous medicine man, he'd been known to steal a dried fish or two, but he had never been cruel.

"Perhaps the ishkodewaaboo has destroyed his heart," Yellow Kettle said.

"And I'll be sure to destroy the rest of him," said Old Tallow.

Omakayas finished weaving a length of basswood twine and set out into the low-growing woods around their camp to set rabbit snares. She wasn't having much luck, and the sight of fat rabbits running here and there, not cooking in their one remaining stew pot, infuriated her. There were lots of rabbits this year, but could she catch one? It appeared not.

She bent over, looking closely at the ground for rabbit tracks or droppings. Quill, who now wore the raggedest of skins and old makizinan, passed her without a laugh. He didn't even tease her about her lack of skill. She figured things must be pretty bad if Quill didn't even laugh at her.

"Aren't you even going to make fun of my snares?" she asked.

Quill crouched next to her and examined her work, but said nothing. He smelled better now that his porcupine was too big to stay on top of his head. The quilling of LaPautre's face had been its last valiant act.

"Where is your warrior animal?" asked Omakayas.

"Recovering its strength," said Quill in a sad voice.

The porcupine had not been the same since it was flung through the air. It was still in shock, and didn't want to leave its human beings. The porcupine stayed in camp munching the soft inner bark of aspen that Quill gathered for it every morning. As it ate, he stroked its nose and murmured words of praise.

"I'm going to catch a beaver," said Quill, still refusing to criticize Omakayas's work. He was turning into a very good hunter and had fashioned a limber bow and swift arrows to replace those that were stolen. He already had taken four beaver pelts, and Omakayas had stretched them. They were making a coat for Old Tallow. If Omakayas could snare some rabbits, she'd make a rabbit blanket for Nokomis. It was already getting cold at night and snow was in the air.

With freezing hands, Omakayas set ten snares, just

where she hoped rabbits would jump. Then she gathered some highbush cranberries. They would be good with venison, if only Fishtail could get a deer.

Such were their lives now! They had planned to reach Auntie Muskrat's camp rich with furs, their packs bursting with manoomin and dried weyass, pemmican, and seeds. Now they were reduced to scratching for survival.

PLACE OF MEDICINES

When Nokomis realized that her medicines and her garden had been stolen, she had actually cried. The seeds were her life's work—each was selected over the years from the corn or potato or squash with the vigorous qualities Nokomis coveted. There was no replacing such a treasure. Omakayas had never seen her grandmother weep before. Old Tallow's face had boiled into a thundercloud, for she so loved Nokomis. Old Tallow had stomped from the camp to deal with her anger. For a time, she could be heard thrashing around and growling in the bush.

"Granddaughter," said Nokomis one morning, "come with me and gather. At least we have everything we need right here."

She gestured at the swamp before them. "What you see before you is a great medicine bundle." She and

Omakayas walked out into the waabashkiki and set to work then, assembling all the medicines that they would need for the winter.

They gathered baakwaanatig, the staghorn sumac, whose furry red berries made a strengthening drink when added to water. Nokomis dried great clumps of these berries as well, for they would stop bleeding. They picked bagizowim, mugwort, which was a good heart medicine. They dug the roots of ininiwa'inzh, milkweed, and collected the leaves of oja'cidji'bik, which they would use to heal bruises, and the roots that cured boils. They collected wiishkobi-mashkosi, sweetgrass, and wiikenh, sweet flag, for colds and coughs, toothaches, cramps, fevers. They brought back great armfuls of reeds for Angeline to use in weaving mats.

Omakayas spent each day of that moon in the great medicine swamp with Nokomis. In her later years, she would realize that this was when she had received the greatest part of her education. She learned all that Nokomis knew. This was how she became a healer.

A FAINT LIGHT

There was frost on the ground in the mornings now. One day, Omakayas walked out into the swamp to check her snares and saw that Quill was gently adjusting each one of them.

He was helping her without telling her!

Omakayas turned away, not sure whether to be grateful

or ashamed. Later on, when she checked the rabbit snares, she saw that Quill's adjustments had been smart, and two rabbits, waaboozoog, were caught.

Omakayas pulled the loops off each waabooz, reset the snares trying to copy Quill's method, and brought the animals home to Mama.

"Howah!" Bizheens was adventurous and tumbled everywhere around the camp. Yellow Kettle worried constantly that he would walk into the fire, or fall into deep water. As often as she could, she gave him some little task, but he was lively as a kitten and slipped away whenever he could to inspect his surroundings. Fishtail was using every one of his bullets wisely. He'd brought home a deer and a runty moose, and Mama had made a new set of skin clothes for Bizheens, as well as makizinan lined with rabbit fur. He, at least, had warm clothing.

Mama took the rabbits gratefully from Omakayas. Her temper had remarkably improved during this crisis. It seemed that she was firmer with herself and more in control when her little family was in danger. And she was very worried about Deydey. She nursed him with tenderness.

"I didn't catch the waaboozoog. It was Quill," said Omakayas. "He followed me, reset my snares, and the rabbits hopped right in. Why is he so good at it?"

"Maybe his porcupine told him a few things," said Mama jokingly.

Omakayas wondered if there wasn't something to what

Mama said. She walked over to the porcupine, who was, as usual, sitting in the corner of the camp clearing with a pile of bark before him. He was looking fat and worried. Omakayas sat down on the ground near him.

"Gaag," she said, "what is my brother's secret?"

The porcupine looked at her with sympathetic, shining black eyes, but of course said nothing. Omakayas touched its nose and it sniffed at her gently.

"Why don't you ask your brother his secret?" asked Mama. But the very thought of asking Quill for his advice was . . . well, it was just impossible! She was the older sister. She could hardly ask for her younger brother's help. She was supposed to be the one with the knowledge.

Omakayas kept setting her snares every morning, and during the day, she was sure, her brother went out and made his clever adjustments. Now there were always a few rabbits caught. Omakayas thought that she would learn by looking at exactly what he had done in her absence, but once the rabbit had struggled in the loop it was hard to tell how Quill had set it.

She went to Deydey. As he rested, in darkness, he liked to have her come and talk to him and sing to him. He was using his knife to carve out a new wooden chess set. His old one, much treasured, had been one of those things stolen. He was carving by feel, and doing a good job of it. Little horses, towers, pawns, and robed bishops were lined up next to his bed of springy fir boughs. He reached his

106

hand out and Omakayas held it as she sat beside him.

"Deydey, can you help me snare rabbits as well as my brother? Can you give me your knowledge?"

"You must think like a rabbit," he said.

Omakayas was silent. What did this mean?

"My daughter," said Deydey, "I have had a great deal of time to reflect as I lie here. One of the things that I regret most, stolen from us by LaPautre, was my medicine bag. I was keeping your feathers in that bag. Also, the stone pipe that belonged to my father and his father before him. I will have to make a new pipe. I will have to travel to the land of the Bwaanag in order to trade for their stone, or I will have to use the black stone that we find farther north. I miss that pipe of my fathers very greatly. And I also miss the four feathers that you gave me. You were so brave in taking them. I meant to use those in a ceremony."

"What ceremony?" asked Omakayas.

"A ceremony that would honor my daughter when she became a young woman," said Deydey.

"But Angeline has already . . . ," Omakayas began. Then she realized that Deydey was talking about his younger daughter. Her face grew warm and she couldn't speak. Deydey sounded sad when he spoke again.

"My girl, if I do not recover, I want you to live a strong life."

"Don't talk that way," said Nokomis, walking into the

birchbark house. "You are going to get well if you just lie still!"

"I am growing weak here!" said Deydey irritably.

"You are allowing your face and eyes to heal."

Deydey sighed, and as Nokomis unwrapped the cloth and the medicines from his face, he said grumpily, "You're going to dose me again, I suppose."

"Yes," said Nokomis, "now lie still while I wash your eyes with my balsam tea."

"Balsam tea, balsam tea, that's all I hear. Your great cure-all!"

Nokomis tenderly poured the warm tea from a clean birchbark makak that she made each time she prepared new tea. Deydey quietly bore her ministrations.

"Bekaa," he said, blinking as she lifted the cup away. "Bekaa, Nookoo!"

"What is it?"

"Nookoo," Deydey said softly, blinking harder, "I can see a little light!"

The leaves fell off the trees in great windy gusts, and the days were cold, but with Quill's help rabbits continued to be caught in the snares. If there was nothing else to eat, there was always rabbit soup. Omakayas and Nokomis dug cattail roots and Mama boiled them and mashed them into the stew. Every day, they added one more item to their store of survival goods. At night, as they sat together around the fire, they were closer than ever in their determination.

"Old LaPautre will not undo us," said Yellow Kettle, "but it worries me. What did he do to those children? And what about my sister, Muskrat?"

"If he harmed one hair, I'll have his whole head," said Old Tallow grimly, gulping at her soup.

She looked ferociously at the spoon she'd carved and smiled. Omakayas thought she'd bite the round part off just to prove her rage.

"I plan to hunt him down one day," said Quill.

The cold nerve in his voice chilled Omakayas. It was as if her brother was becoming a different person.

"LaPautre will undo himself," said Nokomis. "Nothing that you could do, any of you, could possibly be as evil as the spirit of the rum he drinks."

They fell silent, knowing this was true.

Angeline passed around a basket of nuts—she was very smart about watching where squirrels and mice put their caches, and she raided them.

"The poor mice!" said Fishtail, teasing her.

"Poor mice!" said Angeline. "We are in no position to feel sorry for them! We are just one skinny rabbit away from starving!"

But they'd banked their birchbark house well with earth and leaves, and their stomachs were full—for now. They all slept well, even though that night it snowed for the first time and when they woke, the earth was shining and white.

ELEVEN

WIINDIGOO MOON

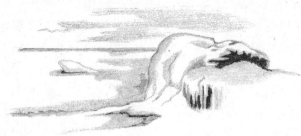

The snow fell early, long, and deep. Five days passed and there was nothing to eat. Deydey sang his spirit songs until he was hoarse, hoping to conjure an animal near or at least pluck up their courage. Nokomis and Angeline ranged the woods for dried berries, more squirrel caches. Omakayas swallowed her pride and asked Quill to help her set snares. But it seemed some magic was upon the land, making animals scarce as ghosts. The porcupine had gone to sleep in a hollow log, a place that only Quill knew about. He was suspicious of Old Tallow, who had joked once about eating his medicine animal. He would not reveal where it slept. Instead, he took his bow and arrows out each morning, though his clothing was now too thin for the harsh wind. Quill bravely went out hunting with Fishtail, and each night they returned, famished, empty-handed, hoping that the women had managed to find something. Anything.

This was usually the time of year when they had wild rice, fish, dried pemmican, stores from the summer to rely upon. This was the time of year when they could count on the bale of dried fish, the stash of mushrooms and nuts, the sacks of fat and berries, even some bits of last spring's maple sugar. All of this had been stolen.

Old Tallow ranged far with her dogs and her spear. Her dogs needed to eat, too. They had to have meat to live. They caught mice, flipped them in the air, and crunched their  bones. As they weakened, she weakened, though she rose fierce as ever and made her way out into the biting wind. She was on the trail of a bear, she said, with bigger tracks than any she had ever seen. It had not yet gone in to hibernate, but was still fattening itself. On what?

One day, Old Tallow came back with a handful of mice, which she threw at Mama's feet.

"I return," she cried with the air of a great hunter.

In spite of their dizzy pain, everyone laughed, even Quill, who suffered terribly from his worst nightmare—nothing to eat. Mama put the mice in the stew pot with some bits of leather, and the whole family choked down the mice-leather stew for strength.

Day by day, Omakayas could feel everyone growing weaker. Bizheens's cries, so shrill at first when he suffered hunger pains, had dulled to a whimper. They all smoked kinnikinnick to dull the stabs in their guts. There were days when she hadn't the strength to move and lay still in her blanket, sick and listless. Every night, she tried to dream of an animal, a place to hunt. But even her dream animals had deserted her. Yet always, Old Tallow would rise and spend her day hunting. Wearing only her thin dress and a ragged deer hide, she would drag herself and her spear out the door with a growl and call her dogs, who would always come even though they suffered too. Sometimes she looked like an old oak tree, bent crooked. But as she strained to the hunt she grew lithe and limber as when she was young.

"Aaargh," she would say when she returned each night, warming her hands at the fire. "I can stand the hunger, it is the cold

I hate! Somewhere around here, a huge bear is wearing my coat. I mean to have it, tomorrow!"

Each day, too, Deydey tried to rise. Sometimes he got past Nokomis and stumbled out into the snow, but then he stood, bewildered and discouraged. Although with each day, each dose of balsam tea, his vision recovered just a little, he could still only distinguish the shadows of things. And in this time of aching hunger, he despaired.

"LaPautre and his big belly would feed us all for a moon!" he said. "I could eat him alive!"

"Saa! Don't talk like that!" said Yellow Kettle.

The dreadful cannibal spirit of the wiindigoo was on the land, the spirit that drove people mad with hunger as it hid the animals and put the fish to sleep. They could all feel its bitter breath.

That night, Omakayas dreamed at last. In her dream the bear woman, her helper, came to visit her. The bear woman was powerful, with a strange face that was both bear and human. She wore beautiful buckskin clothing. Her paws were silky with long, powerful, curved black claws.

"I must take one of you," she said, "but the rest I will allow to live."

Omakayas woke in the dark, dizzy and frightened. She could not rise, nor could she compel herself to do so the next morning. It was as though the bear woman had frozen her. She listened to the others in the wigwam.

Fishtail was too famished and weak to go out. Yellow Kettle tried to comfort the whimpering Bizheens by giving him one of her makizinan to chew. Deydey was silent and Nokomis could barely drag herself about to keep the fire going. Omakayas managed, at last, to help her grandmother brew swamp tea and balsam tea with melted snow. It was all they had. At least, along with the kinnikinnick, it helped with their stomach cramps. Hours passed, and Omakayas thought perhaps she would describe her dream, but her mind was invaded by dread. Who would the bear woman take? She tried to fall asleep again and find her spirit, tried to offer herself, but now her sleep again was black.

Outside, even the dogs were still. At last, from the corner, Quill's choked voice emerged.

"My medicine animal would save our lives. My family, I will get him for you. As my strength is gone, I have asked him for help."

Omakayas closed her eyes in relief. Just a bit of meat, a tiny morsel, and she was sure that she would be strong enough to set more snares.

"Gaawiin," snarled Old Tallow from her nest in the very corner. "He tried to save us, that porcupine! I will never forget how he quilled LaPautre! That brave little creature took our only revenge. He is medicine for us all!"

Slowly, she hoisted her body into a sitting position. Then, crouching, she grinned at them all. Her teeth were long and yellow in the light from the door, her face was shrunk as death. Her skin blazed, white as a skull. There was a mad light in her eyes that frightened Omakayas, but amazed her, too. She had the same look as her bear spirit. Crawling forward, Omakayas tried to stop Old Tallow from going out, but she fell in a faint. She could see her own hand, the fingers like whittled sticks. How could the old woman be capable of anything when even their strongest young men could not move?

"My relatives, nindinawemaganidok," Omakayas heard her beloved protector say, "it is time for Old Tallow to hunt the bear!"

There was a flash of light as she crawled out the door and dropped the bark back in place. Her dogs howled with savage need as Old Tallow called them to her aid. Then darkness, stillness, a swoon of hunger and pain. She was gone.

TO THE DEATH

Hours passed and Old Tallow did not return. Omakayas felt the life leaving her body, though she struggled to rise. She remembered her dream of the bear woman and knew that in facing the spirit of the bear Old Tallow was in great peril. Everybody wanted to go after Old Tallow, but one by one, they tried to move, and could not. Bizheens lay quiet, and Yellow Kettle gave him her other makizin to chew. Snow to sip. Nokomis had nothing for them, again, but tea. At last, after drinking the balsam tea, Fishtail spoke to Quill, gasping for breath. The hand he raised was skeletal. He touched Quill's skinny arm.

"Let us die well, little brother. We must find our grandmother. I have two bullets left. Let us go out and slay a bear! And a moose!"

"I am with you," said Quill.

Painfully, slowly, the two dragged themselves onto their hands and knees, and then they stumbled out the door. They wrapped skins around their shoulders and set off in the tracks of Old Tallow, weaving slightly, praying for strength. Omakayas now rose. Somehow she found the will to follow them. It seemed to her a great surprise that her feet could move beneath her. All she knew was that she must find Old Tallow. When she was a tiny girl, the old woman had saved her and brought her to Yellow Kettle so that she could live. Omakayas could not abandon the old woman who had rescued her as a baby, and who had loved her ever since. Even if it meant that she herself fell dead in the snow, Omakayas was determined to find Old Tallow.

Each step was agony. Omakayas staggered after the hunters, who had found Old Tallow's trail. After a while, she could see, with amazement, that instead of weakening, the steps of Old Tallow had gained strength. The old woman had taken great strides. She had leaped rocks, outpaced her dogs. She must have been carried by the sight of the bear, thought Omakayas. Or perhaps by the bear itself. She could see, here and there, a giant track of the creature that Old Tallow was intent upon slaying.

The wind vibrated in the trees with a dismal growl. Omakayas knew it was the spirit of the wiindigoo and she found the strength to growl back. She asked the bear woman to help find Old Tallow, and so spare the old woman, although she had killed so many of her kind.

But first Omakayas came upon her brother. He was curled in the snow, too weak to move.

"Go on, go on, my sister!" His voice was thin.

She came upon one of Old Tallow's dogs, stone dead and frozen. It had dropped from weakness. Then another dog, bloody, with Fishtail dragging it slowly behind him.

Omakayas knew that Fishtail was going to bring the dog back to eat.

"No," she said, "come with me. We must find our grandmother."

"Yes," said Fishtail. "You are right, little one."

He dropped the dog's carcass and tried to follow Omakayas, who now moved with a strength that was not her own. She saw that her feet were taking step after step. The wind had ceased to cut her. She felt light now and warm. She did not notice when Fishtail dropped behind her, stumbled in the snow, and fell. She was following the tracks of the old woman she so loved. And from their swift sureness, she could tell that Old Tallow was closing in on the bear.

And there it was.

Around the corner, in a clearing red with blood, Omakayas saw a sight that would remain with her all of her life.

She blinked, then rubbed her eyes. Old Tallow and the bear were standing in the clearing together. They were clenched, upright, in an unbelievable embrace.

Omakayas put her arms out and stumbled toward them in joy, crying out.

"Tallow! Tallow! My mother! My grandmother!"

She was sobbing with relief, then sobbing with a dawning realization. The huge bear's face was caught in a snarl, its chest pierced by Old Tallow's spear. Old Tallow's dead eyes stared into the eyes of the dead bear. She was caught by its tremendous claws, which had raked into her neck. They had died together, upright, frozen in their struggle.

Omakayas found herself at Old Tallow's feet, holding the edge of her tattered dress. Darkness took her. Later, much later, she heard voices. Felt herself carried. Tasted a heavy broth. But for a long time she knew nothing. She did not want to emerge. She wanted to stay in the darkness with the old woman she had loved.

TWELVE

AADIZOOKAANAG

The family had been so close to starving that they had to feed themselves slowly. Yellow Kettle started them out with soup and broth, and gradually they began to eat the meat of the bear as well. Each day, as the food entered her body, Omakayas felt herself growing just a little stronger. But nothing could fill the absence that had opened around her heart. She wanted Old Tallow back, and every morning when she woke and realized that Old Tallow was gone, she turned her face to the wall in despair.

Nokomis had realized that Omakayas would be the one most affected by the old woman's death, and she had made her a spirit bundle to comfort her. She had taken a lock of Old Tallow's iron gray hair and wrapped it in some of the bear's fur. Omakayas would keep this bundle with her for a year and offer it food and water when she missed Old Tallow. It would help her with her sadness.

Nokomis told stories to keep up their spirits. She told stories to teach them, to heal them. Nokomis could tell the stories of the old times, the aadizookaanag, because the frogs and snakes were frozen in the ground. So as the little family mourned and recovered, she told stories to help them gain their strength and laugh again.

"Nookoo," said Omakayas one night, "remember how you promised to tell the story of the girl who was a bear?"

She had no tobacco, as that was stolen away, but she put a pinch of dried leaves in her grandmother's hands to request the story.

"Nimikwenimaa, my girl," Nokomis said. "I will tell you the story now."

THE BEAR GIRL
MAKOONS

Mewinzha, mewinzha, a long time ago, there lived an old man and woman who were very poor. They had three daughters, whom they all loved just the same, even though the youngest was a bear. She had fur and long teeth. She really was a bear. They called her Makoons, Little Bear. She was a very good sister, but her older sisters were vain and selfish.

One day, while their parents were out hunting, the two older sisters decided to run off to a faraway village and look for husbands. They tried to sneak away from their little bear sister because they were ashamed of her teeth and fur, but she heard them and followed them. When she caught up with them, they took her back and tied her to a bunch of tough-rooted rushes growing in the slough. But Makoons caught up with them with the pack of rushes, mud, and roots all still roped and piled on her back.

The sisters brought her home a second time, and this time they tied the little bear sister to a

great rock. Then they ran away, sure she wouldn't follow them. But Makoons caught up with them again, and the big rock was still tied to her back. The third time the sisters brought her back, they tied her to the biggest pine tree they could find. This time they were sure that they could get away, and they ran and ran until they came to a wide and turbulent river. On the banks of the river, they had to stop. They stood there, defeated by the rapids. Suddenly, they heard their little bear sister crashing through the woods. Soon she appeared. On her back, she had the great pine tree.

"My sisters," said Makoons, "I am not following you because I want a husband. I just love you, and you can't get along without me. I know things and I can do things."

Then the bear sister took the pine tree from her back and made a bridge with it across the dangerous river. All three got across.

"Now," said Makoons, "we must be very careful. A woman and her two daughters live near this place, and they practice bad medicine. They will invite us into their lodge and offer to feed us a stew. My sisters, do not eat until I do, for the stew may be made of snakes and toads."

Just as the bear sister said, a powerful-looking

woman invited them to stay the night and to eat. Her daughters made them welcome, too. But the older sisters would not eat the first dish the bad woman set out, because Makoons said, politely, that this wasn't the sort of food they ate. Then the bad medicine woman made a new dish of food, and when the sisters saw Makoons eat it, they did too.

That night, the woman gave Makoons's two older sisters handsome new silver earrings and told them to put them on. The sisters did, and the earrings were very beautiful, and everyone admired them. The bad medicine woman's daughters had only crab claws for earrings, so Makoons knew that something was wrong. Then the woman said she would sleep with Makoons, and the other girls could sleep together. Once everyone was asleep, Makoons slipped up to the girls and changed their earrings around so that her own sisters wore the crab claws and the bad medicine woman's daughters wore the silver ones.

In the middle of the night, Makoons heard the woman get up. Then she heard her sharpening her knife, but she knew her sisters were safe.

After the bad woman had come to bed and

fallen asleep, Makoons rose and helped her sisters sneak away from that place. When the woman rose, she saw that she had been tricked. She had killed her own daughters that night, because they wore the silver earrings. Now she was so angry that she took the moon out of the sky, and locked it up in her lodge. But the bear girl was good at finding her way in the dark, and the girls kept going. When the sun came up, the woman was still furious. She grabbed the sun out of the sky and locked it up too. But the sisters continued on their journey. The crab claws at their ears helped by telling them, *this way*, *that way*, and they stayed on the path.

At last they came to the village, which was by a lake. The crab claws jumped off their ears into the water, and became crabs again. Everything was dark. The leader of the village was trying to calm his people. One of the sisters said to him that her little sister, Makoons, could bring back the sun and moon. The chief was happy and offered her anything. Makoons said that she wanted a sack of salt, a sack of maple sugar, and his two sons to marry her two sisters. The chief said yes to everything she asked.

Makoons took the salt and the maple sugar back to the bad woman's lodge. As it happened, the woman was cooking stew. Makoons sneaked in and dumped the sack of salt in the stew. When the woman tasted it she cried out that her stew needed water, and ran out to fetch water. While she was gone, Makoons found the place where she'd locked up the moon, and released it. Then she hid herself.

Soon the woman came back, fixed the stew, and began cooking wild rice. As her back was turned, Makoons dumped the maple sugar in the wild rice. When the bad medicine woman tasted it, she cried out that the rice was too sweet and she ran out to fetch water. While she was gone, Makoons found the place where the woman had locked up the sun, and she let the sun out. Then she ran back to her sisters in the village.

Grateful for all that she had done, the chief forced his youngest son, the handsomest of all, to marry Makoons. He didn't want to, but he obeyed. After they were married, he treated Makoons like an animal, ignored her, never sat with her or held her paw. He made her sleep on the floor while he slept in the bed. Finally, Makoons said to him in a sad voice:

"It is clear that you don't love me. I will set you free of my presence. Pretend we are having a quarrel, and then throw me in the fire. You will get rid of me that way."

So the youngest son did exactly that—he pretended to quarrel with Makoons, then picked her up and threw her in the fire. At once her two sisters, who had come to love Makoons, ran up to the youngest son. One began to beat him and tear his hair. The other tried to rescue Makoons, but the flames were too hot. All of a sudden, the flames died down and out of the glowing coals a beautiful young woman rose. It was Makoons.

The youngest son fell on his knees and begged her to come back to him.

"I found out your true nature," said Makoons, "and I will not have you. I am going home to care for our old mother and father. They always loved me, even when I was a bear."

She had no power anymore. All her power had been given to her because she was ugly. But her old mother and father were very happy to see her and they lived together from then on in a peaceful way.

"Miigwech, Nookoo. I liked that one," Omakayas said softly. She thought of her bear spirit—maybe she had wanted Old Tallow to keep her company. Perhaps, now that Old Tallow was a spirit, she would also protect her. Omakayas held Old Tallow's spirit bundle close.

"I liked that story, too," said Quill. "Except I would rather be married to a bear girl than a regular girl. Would I ever throw her in the fire? Not me! Not Quill! If I had to have a wife (not that I want one), I'd have a bear girl who could hunt for me and bring me food."

"That sounds like you," said Angeline. "Always thinking of your stomach."

"Yes," sighed Quill, eating a piece of cold meat that Mama had given him, "it is good to have something to put in my stomach. Thanks to Old Tallow."

Everyone was quiet for a while, and Omakayas felt her heart squeeze painfully.

Quill kept on talking. "When I was hungry, I talked to my stomach the way Nanabozho talked to his arms in the story. Remember?"

In spite of herself, Omakayas laughed. Nanabozho was the great trickster and teacher of the Anishinabeg, and although he'd helped create the world, he was always getting into trouble. Sometimes he got into arguments with parts of his body that would not obey him. Once, he'd gotten angry at indiyan, his buttocks, and tried to burn them with fire.

"Dagasana," said Quill to Nokomis, "will you tell us a story about Nanabozho?"

Omakayas put some crushed leaves in her grandmother's hand and said, "Someday I'll bring you real tobacco!"

"All right," Nokomis said. "Here is that story you were talking about, when Nanabozho killed his arms."

NANABOZHO AND THE BUFFALO

Mewinzha, mewinzha, Nanabozho was walking along when he spied some buffalo. He was very hungry for buffalo, but he only had a knife, no bow and arrow, no gun, so he had to try and get them to come near enough for him to kill.

"Beautiful ones, oh beautiful ones," he called to the buffalo.

The buffalo looked over at Nanabozho, but they did not come near.

"Beautiful ones, let me smell you," he said.

The buffalo looked at one another and ran a short distance away from Nanabozho.

"No, really, my little brothers, I have heard that you smell wonderful! I would really like to find out for myself!"

So one of the buffalo came back to let Nanabozho smell it.

"Mmmm," said Nanabozho, "it is true. You smell delicious!"

With that, he struck the buffalo with his knife.

As soon as the buffalo had fallen to the ground, Nanabozho's left arm took the knife and said, "I'm the hungriest. I want the fat meat!"

"No, no," said Nanabozho's right arm, snatching the knife away, "I'm hungrier. I'm going to take the fat meat!"

"Wait a minute, little brothers," said Nanabozho, "don't fight. I'm hungry too. I'll divide the meat up among the three of us."

"I don't trust you. Right arm is selfish!" said his left arm, grabbing the knife.

"Left arm is the selfish one!" said the right arm, taking the knife again.

"You two, quit fighting!" cried Nanabozho. He became furious. He was in a rage.

"I'll teach you arms to fight!" He took that knife and poked those arms all over until they gave up. Both arms fainted and could not be revived. Then Nanabozho could no longer hold the knife. His arms were limp and useless. The knife was on the ground with the buffalo. Suddenly the buffalo stirred. It was not entirely killed. It got up and looked at Nanabozho.

"Enjoy my delicious smell, that's all you will get," it said, and walked away to join its brothers.

THE LEAVE-TAKING

Bizheens's round face popped up under the heavy bearskin that covered them both. He smiled in innocent delight.

"Mama! He has another tooth!"

Omakayas put out her finger and felt another sharp white nubbin that had appeared, overnight, on her little brother's bottom jaw. He was using his strong teeth on a piece of gristle. Omakayas laughed. It seemed that he was showing her what his teeth could do. His eyes were on her as he gnawed, and every so often he would stop, in delight, and let her praise him.

When they were starving, he'd been so weak and still, not like himself. Now he was rolling around their wigwam, halfway in the fire sometimes, but smart enough to pull away at the last moment.

"Dress him up and take him out, dagasana, please!" cried Mama.

Omakayas and Nokomis had made him a cunning suit out of the hide of a lynx that Quill had managed to kill. Nobody knew quite how he did it—his arrows were increasingly sharp and swift. After the bear had given strength to Fishtail, he had used those last two bullets to kill well. One killed a caribou. The other a moose, just as he'd predicted. For weeks, the family had rested, mourned, regained strength. Deydey said that his tears over the death of his friend Tallow had restored his vision. He could see as well as ever. He could see so well that he'd managed to snare a deer. Now, with that meat frozen and cooked into pemmican with bear fat, the family were preparing to travel north.

Omakayas shook out Bizheens's little suit. It was turned inside out so that the fur remained next to his skin. Nokomis had cleverly tanned the head and sewed the ears and even re-attached the tail. With his little skin boots laced to his feet, Bizheens was a bizheens, a baby lynx. He was warm as a little lynx, sharp-eyed and funny as a baby kitten, too.

"Giizhawenimin, giizhawenimin." Omakayas kissed him as she stuffed his waving arms and kicking legs into the suit. He sat still and let her tie his makizinan onto his chubby feet. She wound his feet first with warm strips of rabbit fur, then fit rabbit-fur mitts onto his wiggling fingers. There, he was all dressed. He exploded out the door. Omakayas wrapped her blanket around herself and followed.

Outside, it was crisp and sunny. A perfect day for Bizheens to roll and toddle through the snow. Omakayas carried him into the woods, though, and let him play while she made an offering to Old Tallow's tree.

High up, on a bed of fir boughs laced together, they had put her to rest. They had wrapped her in deerskin and placed her dogs beside her so they could all journey into the next life together. Omakayas hated to leave the tree, hated to leave her grave, but there was nothing else to do. Every time she visited, she promised Old Tallow that she would live as the old woman had taught her. Fearlessly, with strength and humor.

She promised other things, too, darker things. She swore to take revenge on LaPautre. She did not blame the bear for the death of Old Tallow, she blamed the human who had caused them all to starve.

Today, she told the old woman who slept high in the branches that they were going to leave soon. They were going north, in search of Muskrat and the rest of their family. It had taken them one entire moon to gain their strength, to replace their possessions, to organize themselves.

Now they were ready to travel.

THIRTEEN

CRY OF THE DOVE

Omakayas helped her brother heap fresh bark and twigs around the log where his porcupine slept.

"Gigawaabamin, neeji!" Quill whispered into the opening in the log. His porcupine was fast asleep and would awaken without his human friends. But his life as a wild porcupine had to begin. Quill waved Omakayas away. His voice was choked with tears and he didn't want his sister to hear his last words to his helper.

Omakayas went to her mother and stood still while Yellow Kettle smeared the area around her eyes with black soot to prevent the brilliant snow from blinding them. Quill soon appeared and quickly smeared his own eyes,

135

too, hiding the marks of his tears.

"We look like a bunch of raccoons," said Quill, perking up as he blinked at everybody else.

The family set out, walking north. They set off laughing, although their hearts longed for Old Tallow. Each member of the family had placed a hand on her tree, her sky-grave, and made prayers and said good-bye. They had spent the last weeks making snowshoes, and now each of them could walk over the drifts without floundering. Even Bizheens had tiny bear-paw snowshoes for his feet and tramped along with them until he grew tired.

Deydey and Yellow Kettle broke the trail. Nokomis took turns with Omakayas and Angeline, carrying Bizheens when his short legs gave out. Quill walked observantly, eyes darting fiercely side to side, every bit the warrior. Fishtail brought up the rear, checking often to see that they were not followed. Never again would they trust the approach of strangers. Each of them expected, at some time, that LaPautre would return. They had furs again, which he could rob from them, and food. By now, his need for rum had probably made him desperate and poor.

But the days went smoothly. The weather held, cold but not unbearably cold, and the sky stayed clear. They reached the edge of Lac du Bois with plenty of provisions. Each day they made their camp early, in a sheltered spot. In their pine-bough snow enclosure, with a crackling fire before them, they ate from their sack of dried meat and drank the concoction of strengthening swamp tea leaves that Nokomis had plucked from bushes as they walked. Even as they ate or slept, however, someone always kept watch. They no longer had Old Tallow's dogs to alert them to danger.

As they readied themselves to leave one morning, Quill suddenly ran to the edge of the woods. Omakayas had heard something too, the low call of omiimii, the mourning dove. There were, of course, no mourning doves around in the winter.

"Animikiins!" she cried, and followed Quill into the brush.

There he was, taller than she remembered, smiling as Quill shook him hard enough to rattle his bones. He wore a beautiful suit of clothing, quilled in sharp designs. And her beads. He still wore her beads. Miskobines was wrapped in a blanket held shut with a silver pin. Yellow Kettle had already grabbed him in an impetuous hug. Everyone gathered around, excited. They dragged the two men back to camp, amazed and eager to hear their story.

THE CAPTIVITY

"The Bwaanag became very close. We adopted each other. In time, they let us go," said Miskobines. "They said they could no longer keep us. Ever since they let us go, we have been following your trail."

"You found Old Tallow's tree, then," said Nokomis.

The two nodded, stared at the ground, but then Animikiins looked up and said, "See, here. We also found this!"

Out of his pack he took Deydey's medicine bag and put it into his hands.

"My relative, we were frightened when we found your medicine bag by the edge of the lake," said Miskobines to Deydey. "What does it mean? We heard rumors and thought perhaps you had fallen into some evil, and we were afraid for you. We have asked ourselves, over and over, why would you throw away your medicine?"

Deydey could not conceal his emotion as he accepted the bag, which contained his fathers' pipe, from the hands of Miskobines. For a long while, he could not speak. He began, but could not continue. He gestured to Nokomis. She was the one who told the others about the raid by LaPautre and his men. Most likely, LaPautre had been too afraid of the medicine to keep it and had thrown it from the packs. She told about their near starvation. She told how it was that Old Tallow had met her death.

When the telling was completed, Miskobines and Deydey put together their sacred pipes and loaded them with fragrant kinnikinnick. Then they sat and smoked. The family sat together, thinking, and soon everyone began to talk again.

"LaPautre and his men stole Zahn and Zozed away from us," said Angeline. "Have you heard anything? We don't know what became of them."

"I heard something," said Miskobines.

Omakayas caught her breath.

"We met a family of people who were friends with the priest who has traveled in this area to gain souls. They said that this priest, a black robe, had argued some drunken men into giving up two white children. He was traveling with them to St. Paul, where they could live with other children in a school."

"Were they all right? Were they hurt?" asked Yellow Kettle.

"I don't think so," said Miskobines. "But I did not see them for myself."

Angeline was smiling a little now, hopeful but also bereaved. Fishtail touched her hand. There were questions, and more questions.

THE LOON FLUTE

"Will you walk a little way with me? Along the shore?" asked Animikiins.

Omakayas's heart bumped, shyly, and her face went hot. She looked at Nokomis, who nodded with a little smile, but told Omakayas that she was not to pass beyond her sight. The lake was freezing cold, but Omakayas bundled her blanket around herself and followed Animikiins. It was dusk, and the wind had fallen. Animikiins held something against his chest, under his robe, and when he took it out she saw that it was a wooden flute with one end shaped like a loon's head with an open beak.

"My brother in Bwaan-akiing taught me how to make this," he said. "He taught me how to play it, too."

Animikiins lifted the flute to his lips. A clear, lovely, hollow note drifted over the ice. He warmed the flute and played a few more notes. Then he played a song as they walked along the shore together.

Meanwhile, back in the camp, the grown-ups sitting around the fire heard the flute. They looked at one another. Deydey raised his eyebrows at Miskobines.

"Howah!" said Quill, getting to his feet. "I'm going to find my brother, Animikiins, and discover how he makes those sounds!"

"No, you're not," said Yellow Kettle. "Sit right back down. Nokomis is watching those two and she will bring them back to camp."

Nokomis was sitting on the shore, patiently watching Animikiins and Omakayas out of the corner of her eye. When she rose to go, they shyly followed her back. Nokomis held her granddaughter's young hand, gently, in her old hand. That night, she made sure Omakayas slept beside her. Before Omakayas went to bed, Yellow Kettle came near, stroked her hair, and spoke softly.

"Daughter," she said, "we must talk soon."

"We must?" Omakayas was confused. Yellow Kettle was usually rough and it was unusual to see this tender look in her eyes.

"Your Deydey played the flute for me, long ago, and won my heart," she said. "My daughter, you must be very careful."

But Omakayas didn't feel like being careful. The low sound of the flute haunted her sleepy thoughts as she cuddled close to her grandmother. Animikiins slept across the lodge, on the other side of Miskobines. For the first time, she wondered if he was asleep and if he dreamed. And then the strangest thought came to her. She wondered if he was dreaming of her.

OUT IN THE ISLANDS

As they walked onto the ice, Omakayas was amazed at the beauty of this lake, its many islands blazing peacefully in the sharp winter sun. In the distance, as the sun rose and light wavered on the glittering surface, dark blue islands rose and floated as if on air. Some of the islands they passed were so tiny it seemed there was only room, she thought, for one person. Omakayas hugged Old Tallow's spirit bundle and wished that the old woman would have made it to this beautiful place.

"I'll put your bundle on the most sacred little island of them all," she promised.

There were so many, each so different, the trees weathered by the wind and water into shapes resembling people.

As they began walking they saw in the distance the threads of several cooking fires. A small band of people had come to camp out there in the night, on an island of rocks and pine. They came closer, then stopped. Omakayas wanted to go see them immediately, for she imagined it might be Muskrat's family. But Quill and Animikiins said they would run there first, quickly, and bring back the news of who the people were.

"Don't get adopted by the Bwaanag again," said Yellow Kettle.

"You must take one of the other men along, too," Nokomis counseled. "What if it is LaPautre and his bunch?"

"They may already have seen us," said Deydey. "Miskobines and I will sneak around the other side of that island, while Quill and Animikiins walk toward those people, waving and shouting. That way if the two young ones are in danger, we old men can get them out of trouble."

"And what about me?" said Fishtail.

"You should stay here and take care of us," said Angeline.

Fishtail didn't look exactly happy about this, but he agreed that someone had to stay behind.

After a while, Omakayas saw the tiny figures of her brother and Animikiins, far across the ice, approaching the camp. Her father and Miskobines had skirted the camp and walked along a far peninsula. But there was no need to take such care. Omakayas saw that the people from the camp came out to meet the two boys, and that they seemed friendly. For a long time, the group stood talking on the ice, eventually joined by the two older men. At last, Deydey came walking back, leaving the others behind. Yellow Kettle ran eagerly to meet him, hoping for news of Muskrat.

"They have been seen!" she cried out to Nokomis, hurrying back. "They are living far out on an island! They are alive!"

MUSKRAT'S CAMP

Deydey made a bark sled for Bizheens, and everyone took turns pulling him across the ice. Bark sleds worked well for hauling packs, too. As the family trudged out onto the lake the next day, everyone walked along quickly, excited to be so close to their journey's end. Everyone felt smaller and smaller as they traveled onto the vastness of the ice. Now that they knew where to go, they did not have to stick near shore, but set off across great stretches of the bays.

As they walked all that day, and the next day, too, the ice boomed around them. Jagged cracks appeared where the wind had swept down to the bare, dark surface. The wind itself grew harsher, stung their faces. Omakayas had to move her toes and fingers constantly to keep them from going numb. Her mitts and makizinan were trimmed with fur from the bear that Old Tallow had killed, and made of the moose hide that the bear had given Fishtail the strength to slay. She squeezed her spirit bundle tightly and thanked Old Tallow over and over. Her eyes welled with tears. The tears froze and vanished before they rolled down her cheeks, leaving tracks of salt.

A fog had rolled out of the trees and covered the islands, a warm wind, a cold fog, the contradictory breath of winter. Out of the heavy mist, the outline of a strong, stout woman appeared.

"Muskrat!" cried Nokomis. "My daughter! We have found you!"

FOURTEEN

COUSINS

"Couldn't she have waited a few days before driving me crazy with her Two Strike ways?"

It was a wonderful luxury for Omakayas to complain to her cousin Twilight, and for Twilight, in turn, to allow herself to confide in Omakayas.

"Two Strike will always be Two Strike. But I'd like to give her three strikes," said Twilight. The two girls started laughing, but went silent when Two Strike appeared suddenly. She always appeared suddenly, jumping into a clearing, running straight up to the fire, or bursting into the lodge.

"I'm taking Animikiins out on my trapline," she said in her hard voice. "I'll show him how it's done!"

"Take Quill, too," said Amoosens, or Little Bee.

Amoosens had become a happy, round-faced, excited girl of nine winters, who was always obedient and contented. She and Twilight, who was Omakayas's age, had to stick close to defend each other when their older cousin Two Strike tried to disturb their peace. Two Strike was just a year older, at thirteen, but she was much stronger than her cousins. And now Amoosens found that Quill enjoyed troubling her even more than when she was very little. He liked stealing her dolls, tickling the back of her neck when she was doing her beadwork, making his awful Quill faces at her. It was as if, around Amoosens, he had become again the old annoying Quill who hadn't been stolen by the Bwaanag, acquired his helper, the porcupine, or survived the terrible starvation of freeze-up time.

At times this was reassuring to Omakayas. At other times she wished she had a porcupine to throw at him.

"You ready?" Animikiins carried his father's gun and wore the makizinan and leg wraps that Omakayas had helped Nokomis make for him. Since moving into the camp with Muskrat and her family, he had not asked Omakayas to walk with him. He had smiled at her, but remained distant. He had not played so much as one note on the flute. But every day he went out trapping and hunting with Two Strike. Now, as the two of them walked away together, talking of where the traps were set, laughing, Omakayas felt a sharp pain dart through her chest. Her throat burned. She turned away from the sight and shook her head to clear her thoughts.

"What is wrong with me?" she said out loud.

"Are you all right? Help me with this mat, will you?" asked Twilight. She was busy cleaning the lodge, hauling out the reed sleeping mats and scrubbing them with snow, airing the furs and blankets, scouring the pots with sand from the shore of the beautiful crescent-shaped bay along which their camp was set, with its well-built lodges.

The birchbark houses were set in the great bank of trees that gave them shelter from the wind. A tall outcrop of stone gave them the ability to see across the ice to other islands, and to watch for enemies or friends.

Muskrat and her daughters had riced every bay they could and buried cache upon cache of manoomin the previous fall. LaPautre had indeed abandoned them, but Muskrat proudly pointed out that they were still eating rice! Two Strike was as adept a hunter and trapper as any man, and better than most. She had provided well for them. But Twilight said she paid by absorbing the occasional blow that Two Strike landed on her and by listening to Two Strike's arrogant and boastful stories all evening long.

"How does your mother handle Two Strike?" asked Omakayas.

Twilight shrugged, but her voice was sad: "I think that Two Strike is her favorite. We depend on her, that's for sure."

Amoosens laughed. "Well, maybe Animikiins will take her off our hands!"

At the sudden look on Omakayas's face, she bit her lip and fell silent. Twilight put her arm around Omakayas's shoulders and shook her gently.

"You should see your face, my sister, as though you had just seen a wiindigoo!"

Omakayas, her heart burning hot with fury, turned away. All of a sudden, she knew what she felt, and it was bad, it was awful, nobody would understand! As she beat the sleeping mats, she desperately missed Old Tallow. Old Tallow would slowly nod, smoke her pipe, and squint her eyes. She would fully comprehend what was in Omakayas's heart right now. And maybe, she hoped, Nokomis would too. But Twilight and Amoosens seemed too young for the feeling that Omakayas grappled with. As she attacked a skin with her fletching tools, as she hauled wood from the bush and chopped away at the frozen haunch of a moose, a blackness rose in her, stark and sickening.

This feeling she had seemed ancient. It was mean, hot, and vengeful. It was related to the way she felt about Two Strike's adopted father, LaPautre. If there was a word for it, that word was hatred.

No, she thought, unhappy with such wretched feelings, there was nobody who would understand what was in her heart.

"Aaargh! Nnnbbbfff!" Around the corner came Quill, looking dejected and furious.

"What is it, my little brother?"

Even though he still drove her crazy sometimes, Omakayas's heart was close to Quill's heart after all that had happened that winter.

"She's *stealing* him!"

"What?" How startling, almost embarrassing, it was to hear her little brother shout what was secretly in her own mind!

"Animikiins is *my* hunting partner, *my* friend, *my* adopted brother, not Two Strike's!" Quill glared in the direction the two had disappeared. "She laughs when I try to hunt with them. She tells me to go home and haul water for the women."

Quill crossed his eyes and made his voice squeaky as a little boy's. "Can I haul some water for you?"

Omakayas had to laugh, and Quill laughed with her. Curious, their cousins drew near. Quill struck a Two Strike pose, head back, lip snarling. "Puuu, the whole world stinks, but I smell so good!" Quill twisted around and looked at his rear end. He spoke to it politely. "Oh, indiy, were you talking to me?"

He put his hand to his ear as if he were listening.

"Yes, indiy, I will obey your wishes and let you speak next time you see Two Strike!"

Now Omakayas and her cousins were laughing so hard

they fell down in the snow.

"Stop, stop!" they pleaded when their bellies started to hurt.

Quill's face darkened again. He sat down on a log and suddenly spoke in a voice full of self-pity.

"So I, poor Quill, must hunt alone!"

Quill pounded his chest with his fist and looked like he was about to cry.

"Have you killed anything, my brother?"

"No," he sighed. "But I can snare whatever moves. I've gotten plenty of waaboozoog. Two Strike says that's a poor game, not worthy of a great hunter like herself. Or my friend Animikiins!"

Quill ground his teeth, jumped up ferociously, and glared into his sister's face. "I'm going out there to shoot something really *huge!*"

"Brother, you make me proud," said Omakayas.

Quill looked at her with sudden pleasure.

"And you will have the hide, only you, my dear sister," he said. Then a sudden thought pricked him. "Maybe you could share it with Amoosens."

He bounded off with a grimly excited look and Omakayas was left behind. Yet her heart was oddly soothed, and she was touched by her brother's feelings, so like her own. As always, he had made her laugh. And he had taken the poison from her heart.

THE GREAT HUNTER

They could hear Two Strike calling with excitement as she and Animikiins returned that dusk, and the girls ran out to the ice to see that the young hunters bore between them the long, dark, heavy forms of beavers, amikwag. Either their traplines had yielded the animals, or they had broken into their lodges and captured them. Animikiins was quiet as they entered the camp. He merely smiled at the girls and disappeared. But as soon as he was gone, Two Strike threw the animals at the feet of her cousins and ordered them in a loud voice to prepare the meat.

The girls ignored Two Strike and refused to touch the fur until Auntie Muskrat had admired and praised each amik. Then, with happy eagerness, she invited the other women to join her in preparing the meat for a feast and the valuable furs to sell to a trader. But Two Strike wasn't satisfied with that.

"Don't forget to save every bone," she cried in a gruff voice full of scorn, looking over Twilight's shoulder. "The amik spirit regards me very highly, and wouldn't like it if his bones were not properly respected.

"And you, Omakayas," Two Strike continued, "Little Frog girl, bring me a nice, hot cup of tea!"

Two Strike hadn't noticed Yellow Kettle or Nokomis, who both came around the corner of the lodge at that instant. They had heard Two Strike's imperious command.

"You should properly respect your relatives," Yellow

Kettle said before Omakayas could move. "Your cousins are not here to serve you. Get your own tea."

Two Strike faced her aunt belligerently, but her face flushed and she said nothing. She was about to turn away when Muskrat held out a cup of the steaming brew.

"Here is your tea," Auntie Muskrat said kindly.

With a look of fury, Two Strike knocked the cup from her aunt's hand, spilling it in the snow. She stalked away, calling for Animikiins.

"You must not let her do that!" said Yellow Kettle to her sister. "Once again, she is beginning to think she runs the world!"

"We depend on her," said Muskrat. "She has saved us from starving. She deserves good treatment."

"But you are teaching her to disrespect you," said Nokomis sharply. "Now hear me."

When Nokomis spoke like this, everyone paid attention. Deydey came into the camp and she gestured for him to come near. Fishtail and Angeline also appeared.

"When Old Tallow saved our family by giving her life for the bear's life, she did it with a humble heart," said Nokomis. "This is the true way of a warrior. Old Tallow hunted for us all of her life, yet never once did she order me to prepare something for her. Everything I gave her, she received as a gift. Never once did she treat me with disrespect. Nor has my son, Mikwam, or my grandson, Fishtail."

Nokomis gestured at the men and nodded. She swept her hands out. "Miskobines and Animikiins also know that kindness is the way of those with true strength! True courage. Two Strike has skill, but her family is good to her only because they need her. What if tomorrow she were helpless? Would anyone allow her this arrogance? It is not good for her to think that her skills are her own. They were given by the Creator, and the Creator can take them away. In time, the Creator takes everything, as we know. Even the best and the kindest, Old Tallow, who gave her life. If anyone had a right to arrogance, she did. And yet . . ."

Nokomis fell silent. She could not finish. Muskrat wiped off her knife and put it into its sheath. She was angry and put her fists on her hips.

"What is it you have come here for, my mother, my sister? Is it your business to tell me how I should raise this child I have taken as my daughter? You have come here poor, hungry, and we share all that we have. All that Two Strike has gathered!"

"Let me remind you," said Deydey, his face tight with sudden pride, "we come here poor only because we trusted LaPautre, your husband."

"We also come here out of love," said Yellow Kettle, "for I missed you, my sister. But your words to our mother are rude. Unnatural. Has your heart frozen this winter, like the heart of Two Strike? Have you stopped loving us, your family? What has happened to you, Muskrat?"

"Aaiii," groaned Muskrat. She plopped heavily down on a stump and hid her face in her hands. Everyone waited for her to speak, and at last she sighed. "I am sorry, my mother. What have I become? This winter has been very hard for us, too, without you, our family. And my old husband, ninaabemish . . . ah, how I loved the old scoundrel. I am sorry I insulted you, Mikwam. I believed that my Albert-ish would stay with us. Even though he was drinking, I allowed him back into our lodge. Again, he stole from us and deserted us. He has hurt Two Strike's heart, for she adored him and was certain that he would stay by her. How alone I am, nindinawemaganidok, please don't despise me. Never again shall I trust that devil. Ingiiwebinidi-in. I have thrown him away!"

Deydey walked off a little way, still offended, but trying to control his thoughts. Yellow Kettle and Nokomis drew near to forgive and comfort Muskrat, but then Omakayas saw her mother nudge her grandmother. Their eyes met in understanding and they gave each other a secret little grin. They moved out of the way as Miskobines approached.

He picked up his step when Nokomis beckoned him to come closer to the women.

"Take a walk with this nice akiwenzii," Nokomis said to Muskrat, making way for Miskobines.

"He'll take your mind off LaPautre," she whispered to Mama. They laughed and signaled to the girls to pretend that they didn't notice when Muskrat took their advice.

ADVICE

After that day, Two Strike couldn't seem to boss anyone around, and as a result, everybody's outlook improved. Except Two Strike's. She sulked and dragged herself off to hunt only if she could persuade Animikiins to leave Quill and accompany her. But he was less and less eager to do so. He always apologized to Quill if he did, and when Twilight asked Animikiins whether he enjoyed working with his hunting partner, Two Strike, he looked at her as if she were crazy.

"I don't think you have anything to worry about," said Twilight, pointedly, to Omakayas. They were gathering armloads of dry branches to haul back to the fire.

"What do you mean, 'worry'?" asked Omakayas innocently.

"I mean," said Twilight, her gentle face suddenly full of laughter, "that you can't fool me. You've been dragging yourself around, you moony-face! You've been trying not to be obvious that you move with elaborate care when you know that Animikiins is looking. Here is how you purse your lips; here is how you touch your hair; here is how you hold yourself up straighter; here is how you walk when you see him approaching the camp."

Omakayas watched her cousin in horror. "Do I really do all of those things?" she asked. "How idiotic!"

"I'm exaggerating a little," said Twilight kindly. "But anyone can tell that you like him."

After this, Omakayas tried to ignore Animikiins and to act normally. But she found that the more normal she tried to act, the more difficult it was. Her actions now felt false. Every gesture a little silly. One night she went to Nokomis, who was sitting alone by the fire.

"Nookoo, may I ask you something?"

"Always," said Nokomis, patting a place on the blanket beside her. Omakayas sat down.

"Were you shy when you met your husband?"

"Very shy," said Nokomis. "It is good. But my child, you are not yet a woman. You do not have to look for a husband. You are still too young!"

"I know I am, Nookoo, but I have these feelings."

"I suppose the time is getting near, my little girl. When you do become a woman, when you do have your moon, I will make your little woman house for you."

Omakayas smiled. She was not afraid. She knew she would stay by herself in the house, away from everybody else, and receive instructions and gifts from the older women.

"Nookoo," she said. "What about Two Strike? She is older by a winter. Has she become a woman yet?"

"Yes," said Nokomis. "But she is unusual, as we know. Your Auntie Muskrat told me that Two Strike refused her woman's lodge. She went out hunting when she had her first moon. She brought back some ducks that day and claimed that her moon affected nothing. To us, your body has power. That is the way we are taught. When your body is ready to bring life into the world, you are a changed being. Two Strike rejects this."

"Did Old Tallow also reject this?"

Nokomis smiled, remembering her dear friend. "Ah no, my girl. You must remember, Old Tallow was not always as you knew her. Old Tallow was not always rough and fierce. I grew up with her, of course, and once she was as tender as you are. In fact, you remind me of Old Tallow."

Then Nokomis added something soft and strange. "I pray every night that the world does not treat you as harshly as it treated my friend Tallow."

"Nookoo, what happened to her?"

But Nokomis merely shook her head and took Omakayas's hand in hers. She held Omakayas's hand for a long time and gazed into the fire.

"Let's wait up for Quill," she said. Omakayas lay down and put her head on her grandmother's lap and dozed as her hair was stroked and smoothed by her grandmother's fingers.

THE BIGGEST CATCH

A little while later, as they were sleepily banking the fire, Omakayas and Nokomis heard a cracking and banging in the bush just beyond the light.

"Help!" cried Quill. "I caught something *huge*!"

Gasping, he fell into the circle of light. As he fell, Omakayas saw the strangest thing happen to her brother. He began to leak fish. Small silver fish poured from inside his shirt, from the bark basket on his back, from his pants and makizinan. Fish slipped from his sleeves and flopped down under his hood around his ears. Then the blanket he was dragging opened and fish cascaded all around him until they stood in a pool of fish. The sucker run had started and Quill had been to the mouth of the mainland river, where the moving water broke up first in the spring. He had scooped up as many as he could. When the sucker ran, they came so thick they choked the water. Each one of them was small, but taken all together they were, as Quill said, "*huge.*"

"Aaiii!" said Mama suddenly. "That was my best blanket, Quill!" She grabbed the blanket Quill had sneaked from her to carry the fish and shook her head sadly as she put her nose to the weave. "I'll never get the smell of fish from it. But my son, even so, you have made me proud!"

FIFTEEN

TWO STRIKE'S PAIN

The sleeping situation was really getting complicated. It hadn't taken long for Muskrat to decide that Miskobines would make a much better husband than LaPautre. In fact, they were so happy together that they decided to build a small lodge for themselves. However, that left Animikiins uncomfortable, for he could not share a lodge with Muskrat's daughters. Without his father sleeping in the big lodge with Yellow Kettle and Deydey's family, he now slept squeezed between Quill and Fishtail.

One warm March night the family was eating near the outside fire, when the issue came up. Twilight laughed softly and said that Animikiins should make his own lodge and see what happened. This was a bold thing for Twilight to say, and Two Strike glared at her. She decided to be equally bold.

"Is there something wrong with us?" Two Strike asked him outright.

Animikiins flushed and looked away. "Well, you're girls . . . I mean, except you."

Two Strike's eyes went wide with shock, as though she had been slapped. Her cheeks went dark. Tears splattered from her eyes as she whipped her head away to hide her expression. Her shoulders were hunched as she turned. But she straightened as she walked away and disappeared into the darkness. There was silence. So that was it! Animikiins thought of his hunting partner as another boy—perhaps he'd thought that he was paying Two Strike a compliment. Omakayas was completely unprepared to pity her cousin, and resented the tears that sprang into her own eyes in sympathy. Why should she care if Two Strike felt hurt? She deserved it. Omakayas looked down at her lap to hide her own expression.

"What? What'd I say?" Animikiins looked at Quill, who gave a what-can-you-expect shrug.

Both of the boys held out their makakoon and Auntie Muskrat dished out more stew. They ate, as always, with ravenous intent. Auntie Muskrat's bannock was charred on the bottom, but light and hot. She was down to the last fifty-pound bag of flour that Two Strike had hauled across the ice from the trader's. Mean and proud though she was, Two Strike never ceased to work to keep her relatives fed. Omakayas was thankful that her Deydey was not like LaPautre. Two Strike had always been a hard girl, but without her own father to love her, or the adopted one, either, she had been forced to the extreme side of her nature.

THE ROAR OF ICE

The ice was rotten and could not be crossed. Yet since it had not broken yet, they could not use their canoes. This was a hungry time of year, a time of impatience. Everybody got on one another's nerves. Two Strike was a caged beast, sullen and furious. She slept outside. She roamed the island like it was a prison. She spent her time breaking sticks and kicking rocks. The snow turned to mush. The ducks and geese had not yet returned. If Quill hadn't brought back his huge load of fish, things would have been much worse. As it was, the family lived off the dwindling stores of rice and the dried and pounded weyass they'd put away from a moose that Fishtail and Deydey had killed.

Nokomis ranged the island and dug beneath the snow for wintergreen berries, for the bitter new shoots of spring tonic plants. Bizheens had become a strong little walker, and followed Omakayas everywhere she went. He could even point to what he wanted and talk to her, although sometimes what he said came out in long, babbling, confused sentences. He was always eager and playful. He terrified his family one day by running out onto the ice, which was just strong enough to hold his weight, but too thin for anyone to follow him.

"Omakayas! Come quickly! Weyweeb!"

Nokomis and Mama stood onshore begging Bizheens to return, but he edged farther out, enjoying their frightened faces. The more they begged him to return, the more excited he grew. Nokomis had thrown a net out and begged him to catch hold of it. Bizheens merely danced around the links of the net, laughing and throwing up his hands.

Omakayas came running and Bizheens laughed even harder to see another of those he loved. Soon the whole family was standing onshore, begging him to return. They made big sounds every time he went a little farther out, so of course he went farther still, delighted that he could produce such excitement.

"Bekaa!" Omakayas shouted to her family. "He thinks we *like* what he is doing! We must all turn around as one and walk away from him. He'll follow."

"I can't!" cried Yellow Kettle. "What if he falls in!"

"Just try it," said Omakayas. Her heart was pounding. What if Bizheens broke through? The lake had underwater currents that could pull him beneath the ice. Yet if one of them walked toward him and broke through, he'd fall in for certain.

"Turn around, everybody," she said, "and walk away. Just act like we are going somewhere wonderful. Talk like we're excited and happy."

"Oooh," said Twilight loudly. "I can't wait to get somewhere that we're going that Bizheens can't come! Can you, Amoosens?"

"Gaawiin," said Amoosens in an undertone, shouting, "I guess not, sister. Let's try to leave him behind. Let's go to this exciting place!"

"Yes! Geget!" Miskobines said. "Muskrat, my wife, let us go quickly to this place we're going, somewhere . . ."

"Somewhere," echoed Yellow Kettle, with a lump in her throat. She dragged her feet and kept her eye on Bizheens.

"Sure enough," whispered Animikiins to Omakayas. "You're right. He's taking our bait!" Then he called, "Hey! Howah! We're going to go now! I can't wait! He's running after us! He wants to come, too! Let's try to get away from him!"

As his family disappeared into the brush, Bizheens suddenly darted forward and ran right off the ice yelling, "Gaye niin! Me too! Me go! Me go!"

Quill had doubled around and now he swiftly swooped out and caught Bizheens, who wiggled with excitement to be carried off to something he knew was wonderful.

"Now we have to go somewhere and have a feast!" Quill said hopefully.

In relief, Yellow Kettle took Bizheens in her arms,

cuddling him. Bizheens didn't want to be cuddled at all, and he made himself a heavy limp noodle and slipped from her arms. But everybody held him in turn, one after the other, laughing in relief.

"Yes, let's have a feast!" Yellow Kettle cried.

"On what, air?" said Two Strike. She grabbed a stick and hit a rock. The stick splintered. She hit the rock again.

"There's a little rice left," said Twilight.

"Meat, we need meat," said Two Strike, brandishing the stump of her stick and looking fiercely around as if a big caribou might walk into camp.

"Bizindaan!" said Deydey. Then he slowly grinned. "Fishtail, do you hear it?"

Everyone heard it coming. A faint and unmistakable honking high in the clear air. Soon, they saw the black thread of geese in the distance, raveling and unraveling against the sky.

That night, although their feast was slim, they ate what little they had happily. And all that night they heard the cracking and groaning, the grinding and shuffling as the ice began to break. It went on the next day. It was an exciting sound, a mad thunder. The booming whip snaps echoed far across the lake and bounced from island to island. The massive sheets of ice crashed up against one another. Close in, starting with the tiniest fringe of black water, the ice began to recede, crackling and tinkling, flailing, splitting, until soon there was a great black margin of water. Then, one morning, there were just slabs of ice floating here and there.

Spring had come, and the fish would be hungry. Nokomis had her net ready and that morning she and Yellow Kettle set it at the point. When they pulled it in at dusk, they shouted from the canoe and the others laughed, hearing their excited cries from shore.

That night they ate fish roasted over hot coals until they could eat no more. Fishtail took out his hand drum and sang. Muskrat jumped up and did a swaying dance around the fire. She grabbed Yellow Kettle, who pulled Angeline up with her. Nokomis brought their shawls out and threw them around their shoulders. Even Deydey laughed, his eyes full of glimmering fire as he watched his wife and daughter. They were beautiful—the firelight glowed on their faces as they whirled lightly. Sparks pulsed into black sky as the logs cracked and collapsed on one another when Miskobines threw on more wood.

"Want to take a walk?"

Animikiins had bent toward Omakayas, asking her this in a low voice, but Twilight heard. Her eyes sparkled at her cousin, but she looked discreetly away.

Omakayas rose, wrapped her blanket around her, and slipped away from the fire. The moon was at half that night, and already up. The light rode the water and brightened the cold sand. The two walked a little way from the camp and sat down on a great beached log. At first,

Omakayas was silent. She felt numb, awkward, strange. Then she realized that Animikiins couldn't think of anything to say, either, and she poked him in the arm. They looked at each other, laughed, and laughed again. Then fell silent again. How many times could they poke each other, look at each other, and laugh? Someone would have to say something.

"That fish was good. I ate so much," said Animikiins.

"Me too. I can hardly move."

They nodded thoughtfully, as if they'd said something very serious. They looked again at each other, smiled a little, then looked down at their feet.

"My makizinan are wearing out," said Animikiins.

Omakayas froze with shyness. She cleared her throat twice before she dared try to answer.

"I could make a new pair for you," she said, so quietly that she was not certain he could hear her.

"That would . . . that would . . . be *great*," said Animikiins. His voice choked and squeaked.

They were so overcome that they couldn't speak for a long while after that.

"I've been practicing," said Animikiins at last, "on the other side of the island, where nobody could hear me." He took the beautiful loon flute from the breast of his shirt and played a few notes. The sound was soft and clear.

"They won't hear you with Fishtail drumming," said Omakayas.

Animikiins kept playing. The songs he had invented were wild and lovely. In the middle of one song, from far across the lake, loons answered in excitement and their song together made a dark and breathtaking music. Animikiins kept playing, now slower, now with a lilting quaver.

Back in the camp, Deydey said to Nokomis, "As long as we hear that flute, she's safe! But the minute he stops, go and find my daughter and bring her back here."

Nokomis smiled.

"Yellow Kettle's father said the same thing to me. I went after the two of you as soon as your songs ended. But I let my feet walk slowly."

"Thank you," said Deydey. He smiled a little, too, and his eyes did not leave Yellow Kettle as she spun around and around the fire.

SIXTEEN

THE WOMAN LODGE

On a point of land across the bay, there was a stand of old sugar maples that the Anishinabeg had looked after for as long as they had been living there. Muskrat announced that it was time to travel to that camp. Now they would meet Anishinabeg from the other islands. Everybody met during sugar camp and tapped the trees and boiled down their own syrup over great fires that they tended day and night. Now Deydey would get together with other men, relatives, and work out their traplines and hunting areas. Miskobines, too, would sit and talk to the older men and find out when their medicine ceremonies would begin and where his place might be, how he could help. The women would find their cousins and meet new Anishinabeg, who came from the southern shores and even from the Plains. Miskobines said that the mother of Animikiins had been a Metis woman from out near Pembina. Perhaps he would find relatives, even cousins. Everyone found relatives and caught up with friends they hadn't seen during sugar-making time.

Omakayas made excited plans with Twilight.

But just before they were to leave, Omakayas came to Nokomis and told her that she'd found the sign she was becoming a woman. It was her first moon.

Nokomis put her arms around her.

"My girl," she said, "we'll go to sugar camp later. For now, we'll stay together in the little house I have made for you."

The two walked down a narrow path, around the side of the rocky outcrop, to a place sheltered by calm pines. There was a perfect little bark lodge, made just big enough for two or three women. It was floored with new fir boughs and rush mats. That day the women brought Omakayas there, all together, and presented her with their gifts. Nokomis had carved a new wooden bowl and a new spoon, which had a little bear on the end of the handle. Yellow Kettle had made her daughter a new dress to wear when Omakayas came out of the lodge. Angeline gave her sister a brass thimble so that she would always be good at sewing. Muskrat gave her a paddle that Miskobines had made so that she would be a good traveler. Twilight and Amoosens had made a handsome carrying bag for her. It was sewn of soft doeskin, and a little red bird was beaded upon it. Two Strike had even made her something—an awl. It was a long, thin spike stuck in a piece of wood. She handed it over and stalked away. The women brought water for her to drink. She would fast for two days, then eat lightly. Yellow Kettle held her, looked into her face, and stroked her hair.

"When you come out of the lodge, you will have a beautiful ceremony. The feathers you gave Deydey are in his medicine bundle, carefully kept for you."

Omakayas hugged her mother and then embraced her sister, aunt, and cousins. They were all leaving for sugar camp. Nokomis would stay with her. All that day Omakayas sewed and thought. When she was tired, she lay back on the winter dry grass outside the hut and stared into the moving branches high above her.

THE GIRL WHO LIVED WITH THE DOGS

"Nokomis," asked Omakayas, "you told me that one day you would tell me how Old Tallow got to be so strong and fierce. Will you tell me now?"

Nokomis nodded. "If there was a name for the story, it would be 'The Girl Who Lived with the Dogs.' This is not an adizookaan, a sacred story, or a magical story. I can tell it to you now. Sadly, it is the truth."

My girl, I grew up with Old Tallow. I played with her the way you play with your cousins. She was my best friend, and she was not called Tallow then. Her name was Light Moving in the Leaves, a beautiful old name passed down to her by her grandmother. She and I played together until we were ten winters old. That was the year the smallpox came for the first time among our people. When the sickness appeared, our village scattered off into the bush. My family went as far as we could. Not until we returned the next year did we find what happened to my friend Light Moving in the Leaves. And not until many years after that did I hear the story from her lips. But that was once she'd become Tallow.

Light Moving in the Leaves was the only one of her family to survive. So you see, Omakayas, she had that in common with you. She rescued you as a baby, for she felt your loneliness within her own heart. After the sickness, everything her family owned was burned. She had nothing left. Some unscrupulous person sold her to a voyageur, a mangeur de lard named Charette who was so evil no other men would work with him. He lived near a long portage, and was hired to keep the voyageurs' dogs and to help carry their packs when needed. He decided to use

Light Moving in the Leaves to lift and carry those packs. He took the girl, saying she must carry for him. He truly thought he'd get his money back by killing her with work.

Charette piled a pack on her shoulders that would have staggered a grown man. It took Light Moving in the Leaves all day and long into the night to catch up with him. She crawled into camp on the first night, then tried to crawl into the tent.

"Get out, you dirty mutt," he cried, striking her with his gnarled fist. "Sleep with the dogs."

She slept outside his tent. At first the dogs would not have her. They had their own troubles. In the morning, the mangeur de lard threw the bones of his dinner to the dogs and screamed at her. "Eat with the dogs!"

Hungry, she fought over the bones. In no time, she grew quick as any dog at snapping food from the air. And, instead of being crushed under the weight of the packs, she grew stronger that summer, until she could carry what a man does. And she was still a young girl.

"Ah," said Charette, seeing she'd managed to crawl into the camp before dusk one night. "So."

The next day, he piled on twice the weight.

Light Moving in the Leaves wept, for she could hardly drag one foot before the other. It felt like her bones were breaking. She snatched berries along the way, drank the water of streams, stole bird eggs. But she could hardly keep her strength up, being fed no more than a dog. But then the dogs began to accept her. They taught her to crack the bones Charette threw them and to eat the marrow. When he found her doing this, Charette laughed, gave her a blow that made her skull ring, and called her Tallow.

Now when he drank rum and caroused with his fellows, he boasted of his dog Tallow, and how she could carry twice what a man could carry.

She lay outside the tent, surrounded by the dogs, and scratched her fleas and licked her sores. She waited for the men to throw their bones her way. They liked to see her catch them, break them, suck the tallow. She was growing strong, but she didn't know it because every time she caught up with him Charette added to her load. If she fell, he beat her with a jagged stick. Her hair was long and matted, and she smelled like earth and fur. She had forgotten in fact that she was not a dog. All she knew of life was that moment of despair every morning when the old man fixed a weight upon her back—a weight that was too great to carry, and she carried it anyway.

Winter came, and she helped Charette with his dog sled—sometimes he harnessed her, too. She ran and ran with the dogs, pulling Charette along the trail. She still slept outside with the dogs. She wound scraps of skin around her feet. Charette would not grudge her one single fur from the mountainous packs she hauled. He gave her a thin blanket and ignored her icy moans. She was just a girl. He was tired of her and hoped she would die.

But she did not die. The dogs curled around her and kept her warm. Charette beat them too, and starved them, but they were loyal as dogs are. No matter how badly they are treated, they serve their master. That winter passed, and then another summer, in which the girl everyone knew as Tallow served her master as the dogs did and never complained, once, when she took up the load that should have killed her.

Her father had been tall, and Tallow grew tall as well. She sucked bones as she trotted along and her own bones grew strong as a man's. Still the old man made

174

fun of her when she snapped a scrap from the air or when he found her curled with the dogs. He kicked her awake and laughed to his fellows, drunk, that her teeth were sharp as a dog's and they should not get too close lest they catch her fleas.

Then there came a day, a strange day.

This was the day Tallow understood that the weight she'd carried had become the weight of life itself. She understood her own strength. She looked at Charette when he threw a bone at her and realized that she was free. She caught the bone in the air with one hand, stood up, and stilled him with her gaze.

She walked toward him. As if in a dream, he stumbled backward. The dogs had risen. They had lined up alongside her and surrounded her as a pack does its leader. They stared at Charette. He cowered and lay flat beneath their contempt. Soon after, he took sick. He became weak and old. Then, one day, the old man said, "Help me, my girl. I have not been so good to you, I know. But I did feed you, something. A little. And I gave you that blanket. I did give you something, you know. Now I need you."

So here it was, the biggest question of Tallow's life. Perhaps the biggest question any of us face.

What do you do when a person who has been cruel to you becomes helpless?

Tallow had to think—should she kill the old man, help him, or just turn and walk away and leave him to his fate?

Here, Nokomis paused. She and Omakayas were silent for a long while, in thought.

"I think I would have just left him," said Omakayas.

"That is the way to kill him without killing him yourself," said Nokomis. "Yes, it is what most people would do. But Old Tallow, what do you think she did?"

"Killed him," said Omakayas.

Nokomis shook her head, slowly, looking into Omakayas's eyes.

"My girl, she did not kill him. In fact, that night she fed him. She was kind to him."

"What happened next?"

"She consulted with his dogs. For a long time, she sat with them. In their mutual pain and starvation, she had come to understand their language, and they understood her, too. The dogs told Tallow that they had long ago taken her as their master, but that she, Tallow, must leave Charette to them. After all, they had suffered his blows longer than she had, and he had worked to death their mothers and fathers, and beaten to death their brothers and sisters. The tribe of dogs was adamant. This was not

Tallow's decision to make. It was the decision of the dogs."

"What did they do?"

Nokomis said, "What dogs do. Dogs are wolves, with some attachment to us. Dogs guided the first human. Dogs know us as no other animal does. They are not motivated by pity. Theirs is the justice of hunger. Dogs knew what to do with Charette. They did it that night, while Tallow slept."

"What did they do?"

"Let's just say they ate well, for the first time in their lives. They devoured every scrap of Charette. Then, out of pity for their new master, the dogs took his bones and buried them out in the woods so that Tallow would not have to do it. The dogs returned and lived with her and guarded her with their lives, as you know. In their presence, she was always happy and when those dogs died, their children served her, then their grandchildren and great-grandchildren. She was kind and fair with those dogs and fed them better than she fed herself. As she became more human, she told me, their language sounded more like barks and howls. But she always loved them more than most people. Better than her husbands. She had no children except the dogs. The only person she ever loved more than her dogs, Omakayas, was you."

Omakayas was still for a long time. Then she said, "I will always miss her. I owe her my life. But saving me was not the reason I loved her. I loved her . . . because I loved her."

That night, Omakayas lay outside and looked long at the stars. She held Old Tallow's spirit bundle. She felt Old Tallow's hard arms holding her when she was very small. Her sorrow was too great for weeping. It was larger than tears. For the suffering of the noble old woman who had loved Omakayas better than her dogs was a mysterious thing. The pain and degradation had made Old Tallow stronger, but also kind to the helpless. Old Tallow had been just. She had known exactly how long to live. When her life would count the most, she freely gave it. She was proof, in her love, of a love greater than we know. For how, in that heart treated worse than a dog's, had the capacity for such deep kindness grown?

* * *

Across from Omakayas's woman lodge, there
was a beautiful island, a perfect hump of
stone big enough for only a pine tree or
two. As Omakayas held her spirit
bundle on the second day of her fast,
she thought she saw someone moving on the island. It was
the wind, it was a woman, a bear woman. Old Tallow.
Perhaps she saw someone out there, perhaps she did not.
As soon as the year was finished, Omakayas decided, she
would place Old Tallow's spirit bundle on that island.
That would be Old Tallow's island, and Omakayas would
think of it as a sacred resting place for her spirit every time
she saw it.

That day, Nokomis told Omakayas many things about
what life would be like as a woman. She told her that she
could not step over streams, guns, or the clothing of men.
She told her that for one year she could not eat berries all
summer.

"I can't go a whole summer without berries!" said
Omakayas.

Nokomis smiled at her. "You'll survive. We all do. After
that, you'll live a long time and so will your children."

Nokomis told her how a woman loves a man and
how a man loves a woman. She told her how her babies
would be born, and how to take care of them after they

were born. She told Omakayas that she must always remain in full possession of her senses and never drink the ishkodewaaboo, or whiskey, that the traders used to steal the minds of the Anishinabeg. She told her how to read the sky and how to cook stews from lichen and roots. She told her how to predict bad weather, visitors, sickness. She told her how to hunt an animal in her dreams. Many of the things Nokomis talked about, they'd already done together, so they also made plans. They would trade for seeds to plant a garden. They would replenish their store of medicines.

"And we will live here," said Omakayas, "won't we? For a long time to come?"

Nothing would ever take the place of her original home, but Omakayas also loved this place. She loved this lake with its magical islands, each so different, and now there was one that would contain Old Tallow's spirit. She loved the mist and rocks, the reefs with their hordes of pelicans, the dark pines with the vast nests of eagles in their branches.

"Yes, we will live here," said Nokomis, "and I'll make certain that you know everything that I know. Let's make something for every member of your family. It's important that you give them gifts, too."

"I still have these," said Omakayas, smiling.

From the striker pack at her waist, she took the bark packet of quills that she had pulled from her brother's

181

nose and face almost twelve moons ago. Omakayas had promised to make something for him, and now she smiled thoughtfully as she sorted the quills, remembering all that had happened in that year of danger and love, sacrifice and surprise—that porcupine year.

AUTHOR'S NOTE
ON THE OJIBWE LANGUAGE

Obijbwemowin was originally a spoken, not written, language, and for that reason spellings are often idiosyncratic. There are also many, many dialects in use. To make the Obijbwemowin in the text easier to read, I have sometimes used phonetic spellings. I apologize to the reader for any mistakes and refer those who would like to encounter the language in depth to *A Concise Dictionary of Minnesota Ojibwe*, edited by John D. Nichols and Earl Nyholm; to the *Oshkaabewis Native Journal*, edited by Anton Treuer; and to the curriculum developed by Dennis Jones at the University of Minnesota.

aadizookaan (ahd-zoh-kahn): a traditional story that often helps explain how to live as an Ojibwe

aadizookaanag (ahd-zoh-khan-ahg): the plural form of aadizookaan

akiwenzii (ah-kee-wayn-zee): an old man

ambe (ahm-bay): come on!

amik (ah-mik): beaver

amikwag (ah-mik-wag): the plural form of amik

Anishinabe (AH-nish-in-AH-bay): the original name for the Ojibwe or Chippewa people, a Native American group who originated in and live mainly in the northern North American woodlands. There are currently Ojibwe reservations in Michigan, Wisconsin, Minnesota, North Dakota, Ontario, Manitoba, Montana, and Saskatchewan

185

Anishinabeg (AH-nish-in-AH-bayg): the plural form of Anishinabe

asiniig (ah-sin-ig): the plural form of asin, meaning stone

baakwaanatig (bahk-wahn-ah-tig): staghorn sumac

bagizowim (bug-i-zo-wim): mugwort

bekaa (bay-kah): wait

bizindaan (bih-zin-dahn): listen (note: "stand quietly" would be bizaan. . . .)

boozhoo (boo-SHOE): an Ojibwe greeting invoking the great teacher of the Ojibwe, Nanabozho

Bwaanag (BWAHN-ug): the Dakota and Lakota people, another Native tribe, whose reservations spread across the Great Plains

Bwaan-akiing (Bwahn-ah-keeng): the land of the Dakota and Lakota people

chimookoman (chi-MOOK-oh-man): word meaning "big knife," used to describe a white person or non-Indian

chimookomanag (chi-MOOK-oh-man-ug): the plural form of chimookoman

daga (dah-gah): please

dagasana (dah-gah-sah-na): an especially polite please

dagwaaging (dah-GWAG-ing): fall

Deydey (DAY-day): Daddy

gaag (gahg): porcupine

gaawiin (gah-WEEN): no

gaye niin (guy-ay-niin): me too

geget (GEH-geht): surely, or for emphasis, truly or really

gego (gay-go): exclamation meaning "stop that"

gigawaabamin (gih-gah-WAH-bah-min): I will see you

giiwedin (gee-way-din): north

giizhawenimin (gih-zha-WAY-nih-min): I love you

gijigijigaaneshiinh (gih-jih-gih-jih-gah-nay-shee): chickadee

Gizhe Manidoo (Gih-zhay Man-ih-do): the great, kind spirit

hiyn (high-n): exclamation of sympathy or chagrin, meaning "that's too bad"

howah (HOW-ah): a sound of approval

indiy (in-die): the hind quarters of a person; also used in the plural form, indiyan (in-die-yawn)

ishkodewaaboo (ish-KODAY-wah-boo): alcohol

izhaadah (iz-yah-dah): let's go

jiibayag (gee-by-ug): ghost

kinnikinnick (kin-ik-ih-nik): a mixture of smoking materials

majaan (mah-jahn): go away!

makak (mah-KUK): a container of birchbark folded and often stitched together with basswood fiber. Ojibwe people use these containers today, especially for traditional feasts

makakoon (mah-kah-koon): the plural form of makak

makizin (MAH-kah-zin): footwear usually made of tanned moose hide or deerskin, often trimmed with beads and/or fur

makizinan (MAH-kah-zin-ahn): plural form of makizin

Manidoog (mah-nih-doog): gods, spirits

manoomin (mah-NOH-min): wild rice; the word means "the good seed"

memegwesi (may-may-gway-see): little person

187

memegwesiwag (may-may-gway-see-wug): the plural form of memegwesi

mewinzha (may-wih-zha): a long time ago

miigwech (mee-gwetch): thank you

minopogwad ina (min-oh-poh-gwud in-ah): does it taste good?

Nanabozho (nan-ah-boh-ZHO): the great teacher of the Ojibwe, who used his comical human side to teach lessons, often through hilarious mistakes

n'dawnis (in-DAH-nis): my daughter

nimikwenimaa (nee-mik-wayn-ih-mah): I am pleased

nimishoomis (nih-mih-shoo-mis): my grandfather

ninaabemish (nin-ah-baym): my husband (with teasing affection)

nindinawemaganidok (nin-din-ah-way-mah-gahn-ih-doke): my relatives

Nokomis (no-KOH-mis): grandmother

Nookoo (noo-koo): shortened version of Nokomis

omiimii (oh-mee-mee): mourning dove

saa (sah): a polite addition to speech

waabashkiki (wah-bash-kih-kih): swampland

waabooz (WAH-booz): rabbit

waaboozoog (WAH-booz-oog): the plural form of waabooz

weyweeb (way-weeb): hurry up!

weyass (wee-yass): meat

wigwam (WIHG-wahm): a birchbark house

wiikenh (wee-kayh): sweet flag

wiindigoo (WIN-di-goo): a giant monster of Ojibwe

teachings, often made of ice and associated with the starvation and danger of deep winter

wiishkobi-mashkosi (weesh-koh-bee-mash-koh-see): sweetgrass

zagimeg (zah-gee-mayg): mosquitoes

A FEW BOOK NOTES

An Ojibwe friend of mine named Delia, from Manitoulin Island, once had a porcupine for a pet. She told me that the little fellow liked to drink coffee and milk from a cup that it held in its paws. Nevertheless, I would not recommend taking a porcupine home for a pet. I would suggest an innocuous and harmless creature like a guinea pig, or at prickliest, a hedgehog.

There were several routes into the fur country of what is now northern Minnesota. Hoping to meet trading partners or other close members of the family, Omakayas's family decided to enter that wealth of lakes via what is now the St. Louis River.

The story that Deydey tells about his father was taken from Grace Lee Nute's book *The Voyageur*. In a haunting vignette, she writes "the laughable tale" of a half-breed boy who seeks his father just as Deydey sought his own, among the fur traders and French voyageurs who so often made liaisons with Native women. That long-ago boy was greeted with derisive laughter when he stepped up to his father to identify himself. I could not forget how that boy must have felt, and imagined that his wounded pride gave a fierce and unforgiving cast to his soul.

Conflict and war between the Ojibwe and the Dakota for hunting territory marked the time this book takes place, but there were also surprising acts of peace and friendship, which presaged the good relationship between the two groups today.

I was struck by an incident recounted in *Being Dakota: Tales & Traditions of the Sisseton & Wahpeton* by Amos E. Oneroad and Alanson B. Skinner. The meeting between the Wahpeton Dakota warrior Running-walker and the Ojibwe warrior Jingling-cloud concludes this way: "The Ojibway chief gave his best horse to Running-walker and a lot of mococs of rice and maple sugar. Then the Sioux and Ojibway mingled giving presents and the Ojibway were brought into camp where they were told where to pitch their tents. That evening, Running-walker invited all the Ojibway to his lodge, while Jingling-cloud singed a deer whole and made the 'chief dish' for them."

The two warriors then thanked each other and declared that they considered themselves each half Dakota and half Ojibwe.

So the fellowship with which the members of Omakayas's family are greeted by the Bwaanag, or Dakota, was historical fact.

Old Tallow is based on a short missionary journal description of an Ojibwe woman who lived near Red

Cliff. May her dog-loving warrior spirit never die!

Omakayas's family ends up together in Lake of the Woods, which is a mysterious and beautiful place indeed. The next book will be set there in the late 1860s, when Omakayas is the mother of twins who get into trouble even more often than their uncle Quill.

I would like to thank my mother, Rita Gourneau Erdrich, for helping me along the trail, as well as my daughters, Persia, Pallas, Aza, and Kiizh. I would also like to thank my editor, Tara Weikum, and Elizabeth Hall for her own work and her support of other writers.

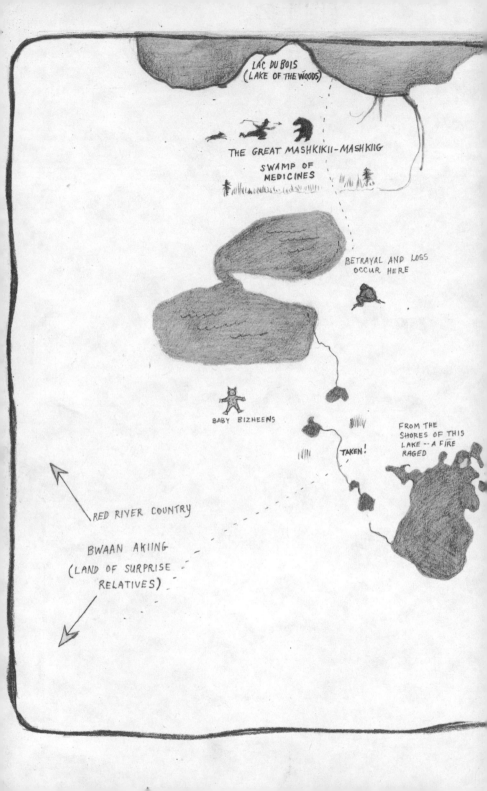